Praise f
Diamond

"The Lucky Diamond is a gem, fast-paced and convincing, with an unusual quest and characters you'll want to know. A great read." Livi Michael, author of *The Whispering Road*, winner of Nestle Children's Book Bronze Award

"A hit for any middle grade readers who like magical quests and fantasy." LoveReading4Kids, UK premier book recommendation site

"A fast moving action-adventure in an amazing world full of magical creatures - and evil - that is sure to have young readers on the edge of their seats." Lindsay J Sedgwick, author of the *Wulfie* series

Books by Valinora Troy

The Lucky Diamond Series:
The Lucky Diamond
Revenge of Queen Rose

Revenge of Queen Rose

Valinora Troy

Revenge of Queen Rose

Copyright © 2022 by Valinora Troy

Cover art by Elizabeth Eckstein

Edited by Joseph Sale

Map illustration by Dewi Hargreaves

Internal illustrations by I. Murphy

First Print Edition

Disresponsible Nodpots Publications

ISBN 978-1-7399903-3-6

To Marvin

Chapters

1. Lucky	1
2. The King Gets Angry	11
3. Sealed Within	15
4. Charlie Has an Idea	21
5. Over the Border	29
6. Underground	39
7. Zania	47
8. The Firebird	53
9. Vicky is Set to Work	63
10. Leaving the Diamond Realm	69
11. Thule	79
12. Prison Depths	85
13. Inside the Palace	93
14. Healing	103
15. Ches	107
16. Fang	119
17. Paul Visits the Prison	127
18. The Dagger	135
19. Fang's Maw	142
20. No Luck for Lucky	151
21. Escape	153
22. Susan's Friend	161
23. Return to Mount Slant	165
24. The Rock	171
25. The Spell is Broken	175
26. Charlie in Trouble	181
27. Suspicions	187
28. Queen Rose	197
29. The Golden Chute	199
30. Alan Enters the Tunnels	205
31. An Unexpected Encounter	213
32. The Third Chamber	217
33. The Sphere	227
34. Escape from the Tunnels	231
35. Reunited	237
36. Explanations	243
37. The Regent	253
38. Battling Fang	263
39. Back to the Palace	269
Epilogue	273

Map of Nivram

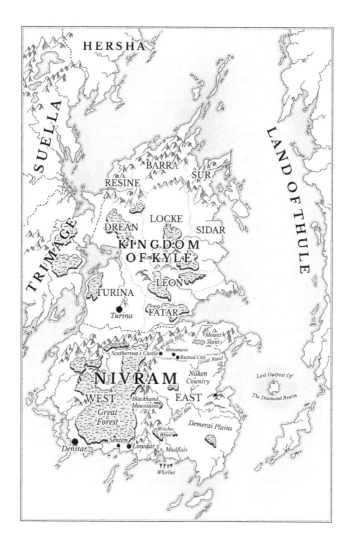

Chapter One

LUCKY

Vicky sat on the wall and kicked her heels against the stonework. In front of her a swathe of emerald green grass ran down to the sapphire waters of Crocodile Lake. West of her ran the long line of cragged peaked mountains, beyond which lay the Great Forest. Eastwards, farmlands, trees, and rivers stretched into the distance. If she looked behind her, she could see Mount Slant. Bathed in sunshine, the countryside looked very pretty, but Vicky, who had spent the first twelve and a quarter years of her life living in city slums, was already tired of her new home. No, tired was the wrong word. After two weeks living there, she was *bored*.

At least in Lowdar, there was always a rooftop to escape over, or a dangerous challenge to tackle. Fighting with the street gangs, persuading the wealthy kids to pay her for feats of daring, dodging the town guards... Vicky sighed. Following the defeat of Queen Rose, Lucky retreated to the Rock of

Diamonds, Charlie disappeared, and now even Paul had left. She had *nothing* to do.

She tugged at the velvet pouch about her neck and slipped out her telescope. The silver tube shone brightly, bringing a smile to Vicky's face. It was the last gift she'd received from her mother, so she treasured it. Especially since she discovered it was magical. She held it to her eye and looked to the lake where the twins played. She could see and hear as clearly as if she stood beside them.

"Alan, be careful, you'll fall in!" Cathy sounded anxious.

Alan stood at the edge of the lake, water lapping his feet. Through the telescope, Vicky could see the sand where the thin roots of the rushes took hold, but then the bank of vegetation ended abruptly, and the lake proper began.

"Do you think if I threw a stone into the water, I'd wake the Guardians?" Alan said in the voice of one keen to try.

Vicky hoped not, for Lucky said that would be the end of the world.

"Vicky! Are you spying?" a silvery voice came from close by.

Vicky jumped and dropped her telescope. A three-inch-tall Diamond sparkled on the wall beside her. Lucky, the Diamond princess Vicky and her family had helped return to her home only a couple of weeks earlier. Vicky rushed into speech.

"No, no, I wasn't! I was only... I mean, I am getting to know my telescope better, like you said. To understand its power." She smiled placatingly.

Lucky twinkled in response. Now that Vicky knew her better, she could interpret the Diamond's different light intensities quite well. She was sure the twinkle was benign.

"Don't abuse it," Lucky said, casting a little trail of light as she hopped onto Vicky's shoulder. "I'm here to see you and Susan."

Vicky returned the telescope to its pouch and slid off the wall, her long plait swinging wildly. She took the Diamond inside.

Vicky and her family now lived in one of the cottages at the foot of Mount Slant, built by the Nilkens to house guests of the Diamonds. Vicky wasn't sure who the Nilkens thought would be staying there, for the ceilings were low, the furniture tiny, and the rooms small. Other Nilkens, she supposed. At least the windows fitted, it was dry rather than damp, and she could enter by the front door. All in all, a big improvement on her last home.

Lucky stood on the wooden mantlepiece, and blazed with light to greet Susan and Yvonne.

"We know the origin of Susan's flute," Lucky said after greetings had been exchanged. "It clearly came from the Thulian people and is imbued with much of their magical powers, the full extent of which we can only guess. Dulstar is anxious to study it in more detail, and I am sure Susan will allow him to do so."

Susan, perched on a small stool, nodded, but Vicky detected her reluctance. She couldn't blame Susan. She wouldn't want her magical telescope taken from her, not even by the Diamonds, who were guardians of Nivram and all who lived there.

"But your telescope, Vicky, is baffling Dulstar," Lucky said.

Vicky was delighted to hear this. "It's really special, isn't it?" Her telescope was clearly the best of the magical gifts their mother had bequeathed to her four daughters.

"Dulstar would welcome the opportunity to examine it," Lucky said. "Although not as powerful as the flute, the mystery makes it a far more fascinating object in his eyes."

Vicky's elation immediately dimmed. She didn't want to part with it. "It's simply a telescope," she muttered, though she knew this wasn't true.

Yvonne was sitting by the table, sewing, but she put down her needle and looked earnestly at Lucky. "Our gifts are so valuable to us, our only keepsake of our mother. We can't hand them over to anyone, not even – Mr? Lord? Sir? – Dulstar."

Vicky was pleased to hear Yvonne's support and nodded in agreement.

"You can be present for the initial examination, if that makes it easier for you, Vicky?" Lucky said.

This was tempting. The Diamond home was off limits to everyone, even Nilkens. "Inside the Rock of Diamonds? You bet!"

Lucky laughed and the dream shattered. "I'm afraid not. But I could get Dulstar to meet you at the entrance. Come up to the Rock whenever you're ready. I must go now. I have some things to attend to."

"Please stay longer," Susan said, getting to her feet. "We never see you anymore."

It was true. Since Lucky had been returned to the Diamond home a couple of weeks earlier, Vicky had only seen her twice.

"Is it wedding plans?" she said. "When are you and Charlie getting married?"

Lucky laughed. "As soon as possible. But it is so long since the last wedding in my family that my father is anxious to make sure it is conducted with all the proper ceremony our rituals demand. Unfortunately, we don't see eye to eye on our interpretation of what is required."

"Oh." Susan sounded disappointed. "That's a pity. Can we help?"

"No, no. Don't worry, I'll soon talk him around."

Vicky wasn't so sure. Charlie had told her that the King of the Diamonds was very stubborn. "I hope you'll allow us into the Rock for the ceremony."

"I'll see what can be arranged. Now, I really must go." With a bright flash and scattering of light, the Diamond was gone.

"Should we go up now?" Susan said. "I'd like to get it over with.'

"All right," Vicky said. "I've nothing else to do."

"If you have nothing else to do..." Yvonne began, but Vicky didn't wait to hear the end of the sentence.

It was a warm day in late spring, with summer rapidly approaching. The sky was a deep blue, and other than a few trails of white over the Blackhand Mountains, there was not a cloud in sight. Vicky set out for the path that led up the slope of Mount Slant but quickly came to a standstill.

"Oh, *thistles*!"

Susan gazed at her in surprise. "Thistles?"

Vicky's cheeks grew warm. "That's what Current says when he drops something or falls over things. This skirt is driving me mad." Vicky preferred to wear leggings, which were far more suitable for scrambling over gutters and climbing rooftops. However she couldn't use that excuse now that they lived in a nice little cottage, provided for by the Nilkens and protected by the Diamonds. To please Yvonne, Vicky agreed to wear a skirt for Lucky's visit but how was she to know the thing would be so cumbersome? She regretted it already. She was constantly tripping over herself in her attempts to stride along at her usual pace.

"It looks very nice on you," Susan said.

"But I can't walk in it," Vicky complained as she shuffled behind Susan. "Your skirt is a much better length, and it's much looser. Why did Yvonne have to make me such a tight one?"

Susan laughed. "It was all the rage in Lowdar before we left, that's why."

Vicky continued to mutter complaints as she struggled to catch up with Susan, and she was more than a dozen paces behind when her sister vanished.

Vicky halted in surprise. "Susan?"

The air shimmered, and before she knew what was happening, a think opaque substance engulfed her and the world around her disappeared. She was encased in a bubble, large enough that she had to stretch her arms to touch the sides, which felt tough and rubbery, though it yielded a little under the pressure of her fingers.

"Yuk!" Vicky said, at the gooey texture. "Susan? Lucky? Charlie? Help! Is anyone there? Can anyone hear me? HELP!"

Her voice was deadened, as though she was inside a giant rubber ball. Maybe no one could see her either. Panic forced its way up from the pit of her stomach, she felt she had been buried alive. How long would she be stuck inside the sphere?

"Let me out! Help! Help!" Vicky thumped her fists against the bubble. It rocked under the force of the blow. Terrified that she would be pitched forward out of control, Vicky stopped moving.

The giant bubble, or whatever it was, stabilised and Vicky breathed more easily.

All right. No sudden movements.

She had no idea what strange thing had attacked her. Queen Rose, Vicky's first suspect, had been banished from Nivram for a thousand years. Had some horrible monster from the Great Forest burst through the mountain pass and found her? It was probably going to drag her back to its lair among the trees and slowly devour her...

"No," Vicky said aloud. "Stop thinking like that. Where it came from doesn't matter right now. How to get out, that's what matters here. Think, Vicky, think!"

Her telescope.

Instantly her fear of suffocation faded when she took out her telescope, a silver rod of hope. She held it to her eye instinctively, and wasn't surprised when the opaque substance cleared, revealing grassy slopes and blue sky above. Some distance ahead, four small cloaked figures pushed a large spherical shape up the lower slopes towards the Little Hills and the border with Paul's land. A splash of blue, like the colour of Susan's dress, was visible within the other bubble. Of course! Someone was after Susan's flute.

She didn't recognise the four creatures taking her sister away. Not Nilkens, Vicky was sure of that, and not human either. She tapped the wall of the bubble lightly with her telescope. Nothing happened. She tried it again, harder, and the sphere yielded slightly, but no matter how hard she hit it, the skin did not break.

A check through her telescope showed the other sphere had reached the rocks and boulders of the Little Hills. Soon it would be out of sight. Which meant there was only one thing for Vicky to do.

Follow it.

"Don't worry, Susan," Vicky said, although it was impossible for her sister to hear. "We're coming after you." It was silly to say *we* when it was just her, but it made Vicky feel better.

Vicky placed her hands straight ahead of her, resting against the bubble's skin. Her flesh crawled at its touch, but she gave it a little push as she stepped forward.

The giant ball, with Vicky inside, rolled forward.

Vicky tried not to get too excited. After all, she couldn't see a thing, she reminded herself, taking another step.

The bubble rolled on.

She took another quick peek through her telescope in time to see Susan's sphere disappear over a ridge.

"Thistles!" Vicky muttered. She'd never catch up. At a loss of what to do next, she rested the telescope against the wall.

The bubble moved smoothly across the grass.

Keeping one end of her telescope pressed to the bubble, and her eye against the other, Vicky stepped forward. The sphere glided across the ground. Keeping her balance became more difficult once she left the smooth turf for the rougher terrain of the lower slopes. If her hand slipped, the telescope lost contact with the bubble and it stopped moving. Soon her arm ached, and only the thought of Susan's predicament kept her going.

Eventually she gained the ridge where last she had seen Susan. Ahead, the ground fell and then rose again in a series of ridges stretching towards a distant horizon. Susan had vanished from sight, so Vicky pressed on.

As long as she kept her telescope pressed against its skin, the sphere rolled faster. All she had to do was keep her balance. After a while, she stopped looking out, and left it to her magical telescope to find a safe path.

After several hours passed, Vicky regretted her impulsiveness. She should have gone straight for the Rock of Diamonds and told Lucky. Now she could end up following the other sphere for days, weeks even, without reaching Susan. In the meantime, she would slowly starve to death inside the sphere. Or die of thirst. Or, even worse—Vicky felt sick at the idea—suppose the air ran out? She would quickly suffocate.

This horrible thought made her stop, but the sphere rolled on and she had to walk with it or fall over. She looked through the telescope and instantly hope revived. She was cresting a hill and ahead, on the next summit was a large grey ball, which hovered momentarily before disappearing from view.

Susan had crossed into the Kingdom of Kyle. Vicky kept looking through her telescope as the sphere passed into the final depression and ascended the last ridge. Ahead was a blackened valley, shrouded in shadow, with no sign of Susan or her captors.

Vicky, reluctant to go any further, stopped in her tracks, but the sphere continued to roll. Vicky lost her footing and fell backwards, dropping the telescope. The sphere rolled forward and plunged down the treacherous slope at an ever-increasing speed until it dropped down into darkness.

Chapter Two

THE KING GETS ANGRY

Lucky and her father were in the outer chamber of the Rock of Diamonds. The King of the Diamonds was shorter and broader than his daughter. At the moment splinters of light shot out from every facet of the king, breaking into a rainbow of colours as they hit the chamber walls.

"We haven't had a Diamond wedding in centuries," he said. "Considering it's my daughter who is involved, I insist it is done the traditional way, in the Prism antechamber."

"Will you allow the children attend it there?" Lucky remained stationery while her father rotated and fumed.

"Of course not," the king roared. "It's impossible."

"Then we'll have to hold the ceremony here in the outer cavern."

"But look at it! It's so dingy." The colours of the king's ire separated into indigos, reds, and oranges before drifting to the ground. So much light shot out of him that the roof of the cavern, with its hundreds of Diamonds resting on the ceiling like a star-filled sky, were almost unnoticeable. They sang softly.

"Simple. Dignified. Exactly what I'm looking for." Lucky paused. "What was that?"

"Nothing."

The singing stopped. Lucky glanced towards the entrance of the Rock; a small archway filled with daylight. Something was wrong. Lucky hurried towards the entrance, her father grumbling as he followed.

The arch of light stretched taller as Lucky approached, and a few Diamonds stood before it, gazing upwards. One of these moved to meet Lucky. Both his voice and body shook as he spoke.

"The entrance is sealed."

Lucky glanced sharply at him and then at the arch. Through it she could see the blue sky with tendrils of cloud, Crocodile Lake, and the surrounding countryside below.

The same view greeted her every day.

Yet there was something different about it, as if the picture was slightly out of focus.

She moved forward and immediately an unseen substance blocked her exit. She pressed a little harder, it yielded for a moment but then held firm.

"What is it, Lucky?" The king peered at her. "An invisible barrier?"

"Yes, Father." Lucky turned to the Diamonds standing close by. "Shimmer, check all the other exits to the sky." He nodded and sped away. "Someone fetch Dulstar. We need his knowledge."

"Preposterous," the king said. "I won't stand for it."

"Wait," Lucky said. Her father was impetuous. "We need to know exactly what we're dealing with before we take action."

The king turned a deep indigo.

"This," he said, "is my domain. *No-one* may attack it."

"It looks like Thulian magic," Lucky said thoughtfully. "As far as I can recall, the Thulians built safeguards and traps into their enchantments, though I cannot remember exactly what. But Dulstar probably will…"

"Dulstar!" The king snorted. "I'm not waiting while he trawls through a few centuries of dusty old histories."

He turned to the archway and before Lucky could stop him, a bolt of light flashed from the king and hit the invisible barrier with a forceful crack. The view trembled briefly, before a bullet of light flashed back from it directly into the king.

Lucky saw her father fall to the ground, his light extinguished, leaving only a pale green opalescence to illuminate his form. She dropped to the ground beside him.

"He's still alive." Relief saturated her voice. "Quickly! Take him to the healing room. Call as many as you can to help us bring him back."

One of the shocked Diamonds stammered. "How could anything hurt the king? Surely Thulian magic isn't that strong?"

"His own magic did this." Too late Lucky remembered the extra features that the Thulians liked to add to their spells. "The barrier reflected back most of his charge."

As they carried the unconscious king away the healing chamber, Lucky wished she had borrowed Susan's flute earlier that day. All her powers might not be enough to save her father from his own spell.

Chapter Three

SEALED WITHIN

Alan had no intention of waking the guardians, he just longed to see them. It was obvious he wouldn't catch a glimpse at the edge of the lake so he waded back to shore.

Cathy greeted him with a smile. She was the same age as him, and, at only ten years old, still the same height.

"Did you see anything?" Cathy was as curious as he was.

Alan shook his head. "Nope. It's like when Charlie took us sailing across the lake, it's a solid blue mirror."

It was a mild spring morning, with only a few white clouds in the sky moving lazily at the behest of a gentle breeze. Since the twins had left Lowdar, only a few short weeks ago, life had become one big adventure, which hadn't ended with the defeat of Queen Rose. Paul taught the twins to fence, and they had enjoyed several epic duels on the rooftop of Princess Scatherina's castle. Tremere, their new friend and long-lost uncle, had taken them to spend the night in the castle and they spent hours playing there. That was on the way back to the

Great Forest for another visit. Tremere showed them how to recognise signs of monsters in the forest, and pointed out wild plants which were safe to eat or more often, deadly poisonous.

Alan would miss Paul, who had left for home that morning accompanied by Tremere. Paul's astronomy lessons meant Cathy mastered the names of the stars, while Alan enjoyed teasing the prince in the Forest over his obvious fear of the place.

Alan picked up a pebble and spun it across the water. It skimmed across the surface, causing little pools of water to erupt momentarily.

"Wow," Alan said, watching the skimming stone continue across the vast expanse of the lake until it disappeared into its blue horizon. "I'm good at this."

Cathy sounded alarmed. "Don't wake them, Alan."

Alan shrugged, so Cathy would know he was not bothered either way, though secretly he was a little wary of disturbing the guardians himself. He started to walk along the lake shore, away from the Nilken cottages and Mount Slant. Cathy fell into step beside him.

"I think we should go back into the forest," he said. "On our own this time."

"No thanks," Cathy said with a shudder. "But I would like to go back to see Scatherina's castle again. We didn't get to see it all."

Her suggestion appealed to Alan. "Maybe some of the monsters from the Great Forest would attack us there, so we'd have to fight."

Cathy looked nervous.

"Couldn't we make friends with them instead?"

"Sure." Alan didn't mind.

Alan's fear that Tremere, the twins' kindly friend from the forest, would transform into Tremere the strict guardian turned out to be unfounded. Tremere remained the same despite their newfound relationship. He even taught the twins to use bows and arrows. Yvonne wasn't pleased but she couldn't say anything. After a morning of practice with his bow, Alan's arm ached. He left his target, one of the few slim trees near the shores of the lake, festooned with arrows, a larger littering gathered at its roots.

"I'm hungry, it must be time for lunch. Let's go back to the cottage and get some food," Cathy said. "Race you."

Alan could never resist a challenge. He jumped to his feet and tore up the slope, Cathy a little way behind him. Ahead, immediately beyond the cottages, he could see his sisters. Vicky stumbled a little in her long skirts while Susan waited for her to catch up.

Unexpectedly first Susan, and then Vicky, vanished. Alan came to an abrupt stop. Cathy, immediately behind, cannoned into him.

She gasped and clutched his sleeve.

"Where did they go?"

Alan stared ahead, his mouth open in surprise. "Could the flute turn them invisible? Are they playing a trick on us?"

It didn't seem likely but what else could have happened? The twins ran towards the place they had last seen their sisters, but neither Susan nor Vicky appeared.

They headed towards the cottage. Alan kept his eyes on the ground in case it cracked open to swallow them too.

The front door of the cottage was closed. When Alan reached for the door, his fingers stopped three inches short.

"What's wrong?" Cathy said.

"I can't reach it." His fingers splayed out mid-air.

Cathy tried but couldn't touch the door either.

Alan dropped to his knees and felt around the base of the door. "No good. It goes right to the ground."

"The window!" Cathy said.

The same strange substance coated the cottage completely, preventing them getting inside. Alan rapped on it but his knuckles made no sound. He picked up a sharp-edged stone to scratch the barrier but couldn't make a mark.

"Yvonne," Cathy shrieked.

Yvonne appeared at the window, her mouth opened and closed and she waved her hands about but Alan couldn't hear a word.

The barrier blocked out sound too.

Yvonne seized the window handle, lifted it, and pushed until her face went red but the window wouldn't budge, dashing any hope it could it be opened on the inside. Then she pointed towards the front door, and raised her hands in a despairing gesture, which Alan understood meant the door was stuck on her side too.

"We're going for Lucky," Alan said, pointing to Cathy and then Mount Slant, hoping Yvonne understood.

Yvonne nodded and waved goodbye.

The path to the Rock of Diamonds halfway up Mount Slant was narrow and steep. Luckily the twins were fit and it would not take them long to reach Lucky. The area was strangely deserted. Usually two or three Nilkens were on the move running various errands of the Diamonds, their cheerful faces beaming at the twins as they went on their way. Nilkens also should have appeared to stop the twins reaching the Rock.

Alan suspected the Nilkens had disappeared too.

From the shores of Crocodile Lake, the entrance to the home of the Diamonds, a huge archway cut into the side of the mountain, glittered like a star-filled sky. From halfway up the path, the archway had shrunk to a third of its original size. By the time the path opened onto a wide plateau, two-thirds of the way up the mountain, Alan felt quite red in the face. Another shock awaited them. The entrance to the Diamond caverns was no higher than six inches from the ground.

"It wasn't like this last time," Alan said.

He dropped to the ground and tried to peer in but couldn't see anything.

"What will we do?" Cathy sounded devastated.

"Should we go after Tremere?" Alan said, disappointed there was no sign of Lucky. He couldn't think of what else to do.

"What's up?" A new voice said. Something sparkled from a ledge above Alan's head.

"Charlie?" Since Charlie the Canoe had resumed his Diamond shape, Alan was never certain that he recognised him.

"In shape," the Diamond said cheerfully. "I'm surprised to see you two here. The Nilkens are usually good at dissuading visitors." Dazzling in the sun, Charlie hopped down to a lower ledge. "Not that I mind, of course. It's the king who won't be pleased."

"Something weird is going on," Alan said. "The entrance to the Rock has shrunk. Look how tiny the archway is now."

Charlie dropped onto Cathy's shoulder. "Of course. You're not invited."

"We're afraid the Diamonds are blocked inside Mount Slant, like Yvonne is," Cathy burst out. "Susan and Vicky disappeared so we thought…"

"Hold on a second," Charlie said. "Could you run that past me again? Yvonne is locked where? What happened to Susan and Vicky?"

Between them, Alan and Cathy told Charlie what had happened. Although Charlie's expression was not as easy to read as Lucky's, when he spoke he sounded serious.

"Put me on the ground, will you, Cathy? Let's see if I can get into the Rock."

Cathy placed Charlie right at the entrance. For a moment, the archway quivered. Charlie stopped short.

"I can't get any closer to it. Hmm."

"What does it mean, Charlie?"

"It's magic, Alan. An enemy has attacked. Lucky, the king, and the rest of the Diamonds are trapped inside. Take it from me, we're in deep trouble."

Chapter Four

CHARLIE HAS AN IDEA

"What enemy?" Alan demanded. He thought Lucky had only one enemy, and she had been vanquished.

"Queen Rose?" Cathy breathed. "It can't be."

Alan agreed. He hadn't been present when the King of the Diamonds had defeated Queen Rose but Vicky and Paul had both told him about it. Paul's version had put more emphasis on the importance of his own role, but both had agreed that Queen Rose had been banished from Nivram.

A short flash of light meant Charlie was shaking his head. Or nodding. Alan couldn't be sure which.

"My history and geography are rusty, but I think I recognise this magic," Charlie said. "Thulian."

"Thulian magic?" Alan said. He hadn't heard of it.

Charlie gave another flash of light. "Yes. It's pretty strong, I can't break it."

"Surely Lucky can?" Cathy cried.

"Possibly. With time."

"What about the king?" Alan had heard how the King of the Diamonds had dramatically beaten Queen Rose. He wished he had been there to see it. "Surely he can?"

"He doesn't have much patience," Charlie said. "Thulian magic is quite complex."

"So what do we do?" Alan said.

"Of course, I could be wrong, but who else would dare assault the Rock of Diamonds?" Charlie mused. "Nevertheless, the Rock is sealed, Susan and Vicky snatched, our Nilken guards vanished..."

"Don't forget Yvonne," Cathy said.

"And Yvonne stuck inside her home, like Lucky." Charlie peered at the entrance to the Diamond realm. "I wonder if she can see me?" No answering glimmer appeared on the other side of the barrier.

"Isn't there anything we can do?" Cathy said.

"Thulian magic can only be broken by Thulian magic. That's why it will take time for Lucky or Dulstar, or the king for that matter, to break it. Of course! That's the solution."

"What is?" Alan and Cathy spoke together.

"The Lost Flute of Thule. Isn't Dulstar studying it at the moment? That will break it in a flash."

"Susan has it," Cathy said. "She hasn't given it to Dulstar yet."

"That's a pity." Charlie sounded disheartened. "Maybe that's why they kidnapped Susan."

"Why don't we go to these Thulians and demand the release spell?" Alan said, remembering how that had worked for Cathy.

"Not that easy," Charlie said. "For one thing, all the Thulians are gone. Except Queen Rose, of course, but it can't be her, she's banned from Nivram..."

"Couldn't she get someone to cast the spell for her?" Alan said.

"No, Thulian magic can only be cast by Thulians. Or possibly Diamonds like Lucky," Charlie said. "Let me think... This attack *has* to come from Witch Rose somehow, she is the last of the Thulians. How she managed it, I don't know. I can only think of one place we can turn to for help. *If* the Nuones are willing or able to help."

"So we ask these Nuones for the spell?" The Diamonds and his sisters were in trouble, and Alan ached to do something to help.

"Wait a minute," Charlie said. "I don't think Lucky would be in favour of this journey..."

"Are you *scared* of Lucky?" Alan said.

"Nothing as much as you are." Charlie seemed a little displeased by the question. "But she will expect me to take care of you, not lead you into jeopardy."

"Is it *very* dangerous?" Cathy said anxiously.

"There's only us to do it," Alan said seriously. "I don't want to wait around here to be caught as well."

"There's something in what you say, Alan," Charlie said. "But let's not be hasty."

"*You* said there is only one place we could go for help," Alan reminded him. "We're willing to go there."

"It's a long shot..." Charlie said, sparkling uneasily.

"Why don't I ask my compass?" Cathy said, lifting a chain from about her neck and popping open the lid of the compass. "If it points to the Nuones, we'll go. If not, we stay here until Lucky figures a way out."

"All right," Charlie said. He sounded relieved.

Cathy pulled at the chain around her neck and opened the compass, which glittered in the sun. Alan knew that it never failed to point her in the right direction, any time she was unsure. If she was to remain put, the dial would spin ceaselessly.

She clasped it in her hand. "Which way should we go?"

The dial began to spin.

"Which direction are the Nuones, Charlie?" Alan said.

"South-east from here," Charlie said.

Cathy held out the compass.

It pointed south-east. Alan was glad. It was up to him and Cathy to save their family, and he trusted the compass as much as Cathy did. He liked the idea of heroically saving everyone, especially the Diamonds.

"Give me a moment to leave a message for Lucky, and then we'll be off," Charlie said.

Charlie made a few scratches on the rock, invisible to Alan's eye, and then hopped onto Cathy's shoulder.

"Can we tell Yvonne where we're going?" she said.

"Of course you can," Charlie said,

As they descended the path, Alan kept an eye out for any sign of further attack and especially for any Nilkens who hadn't disappeared.

"Where do these Nuones live?" Cathy said. Her trust in her compass was so great that she sounded almost cheerful. "Are they like Nilkens?"

"Em, no," Charlie said. "They live in Thule. Remember Lucky told you the story of Witch Rose, how she was ambitious to learn a lot of magic? She wasn't the only one of her kind to want to become as powerful as Thule himself. After Thule banished her and the other Thulians, he gave the land of Thule over to distant relatives, known as Nuones, who were servants of the Thulians."

Alan felt a key part of the story was missing. "Who is Thule? I thought it was a place?"

"The guardians gave Nivram and Kyle and a few other places over to our care, and they gave lands across the sea to Thule, but we know it as the land of Thule, Thule for short."

It was confusing to call the land the same name as its guardian, but Alan understood now.

"So we're going across the sea to the land of Thule to meet the Nuones and ask for their help in breaking a Thulian spell?" he said, trying to hide his excitement at such a journey.

"Exactly," Charlie said. "The Nuones will have some limited knowledge, which might be enough."

Back at the cottage, Yvonne brightened when she saw Charlie, who tried to break through the barrier, saying it looked less complex, but he didn't succeed.

Alan and Cathy then tried to convey the plan, using their hands, which only confused Yvonne further. Charlie shot off a few sparks and Yvonne gave a thumbs up.

Alan wondered what she thought they were doing but he waved goodbye and they set off on their journey.

"How do we get to Thule?" Cathy said.

"We need to go to one of the towns on the coast and arrange a boat. Let's see... it takes me about a day and half to get there. I fly at least six times faster than you walk, so it will take you nine days."

"Can't you fly us?" Alan said.

"I'm not a canoe any longer, and I was never supposed to fly passengers. However, I did receive permission to do so recently ... And it's not like I'm really breaking the shape changing rule either," Charlie said, smiling.

Charlie insisted they started their journey by walking towards one of the Nilken farms. "It's only a couple of furlongs, it won't take long."

"Why don't you fly us there?" Alan had flown only once in Charlie and he had loved it even more than sailing. "It would be faster."

"Let's get those limbs of yours loosened up, there will be plenty of walking ahead," Charlie said.

For a while they walked in silence, Alan pondering Charlie's story.

So the Diamonds weren't the only powerful species around. What kind of creature was Thule, and what would happen if they met him? Alan didn't think Queen Rose sounded so terrifying, but how had she cast a spell on the Diamonds when she was banished from Nivram?

The afternoon sun was warm, and Alan grew thirsty. Before he could complain, Cathy gave a gleeful shout.

"I see a Nilken farmhouse."

Surrounded by shoulder-high grains, the cottage was barely visible, but Cathy's eyes had not misled her.

Current was not at home but his mother, Almond, happily welcomed them. When Charlie told her that they were off on a week's journey and needed supplies, the cheerful Nilken was only too keen to help. Alan's eyes glistened at the quantity of food Almond piled on the kitchen table, but Charlie reminded him that he would not be able to carry it all.

"I thought you'd be carrying us?" Cathy whispered.

"All the more reason to leave it behind. Carrying passengers is awfully tiring. We only need enough to get us to the town on the coast. And two days beyond for Thule," Charlie said firmly. "Now, what else do we need?"

"Something to drink," Alan suggested.

Charlie asked Almond for some blankets and firewood, as well as four canisters of water.

"It gets very cold at night," he reminded the twins.

They did not delay in the Nilken's home, stopping long enough to pack up the provisions, and have a quick lunch. Then Charlie told Almond what had happened, and asked her to warn other Nilkens to be on high alert.

Once on the road and out of sight of the Nilken's cottage, Charlie said, "I'm ready now."

A large canoe with a smiling face and four large feet, the form Alan had first known Charlie, stood awkwardly beside him. Alan scrambled into the canoe and pulled Cathy in after him.

Charlie took a few steps at a fast pace and launched himself forward. Alan felt his stomach lurch, a momentary dizziness, and then the breeze in his face.

They were airborne.

Chapter Five

OVER THE BORDER

Earlier that day, Paul set out for the Kingdom of Kyle. According to Lucky, he had been away from his home for three months, although he only remembered the last two or three weeks since he had been rescued from a hideous enchantment. The effrontery of those who trapped him! His new friends were not interested in his complaints, so Paul had swallowed his outrage, but now he was on the way home, he looked forward to telling his regent all about it.

Strangely, however, Reece still hadn't come looking for him.

His path through the Little Hills rose steeply to the border between Nivram and Kyle, and he was eager for his first glimpse of his kingdom.

Arriving at the summit, he felt a pang of disappointment. Instead of the fertile valley he'd expected he found a blackened gorge. All the vegetation had been destroyed, and even the waterways were dried up.

Tremere stood beside him, gazing ruefully at the scene before starting down the slope.

"Take care," Tremere warned. "Watch out for the loose rubble."

As Paul picked his way after Tremere, his mood improved. He had been reluctant to leave the company of his new friends and that of the jovial Nilkens, but after all, he was returning to his home for a short while. Merely to prepare himself for Lucky and Charlie's wedding, so that he could come back with a suitable retinue. A dazzling retinue, he thought, one sure to impress all with its magnificence. What was the advantage of being the prince and heir of a country if he couldn't occasionally flaunt it?

The sun didn't reach the valley and despite his exertion Paul felt cold. He was glad to reach the valley floor, even though it lay in shadow.

Tremere consulted a note scrawled on a piece of bark. Paul could make out the fiery letters that Charlie had etched on it before Tremere put it away.

"We should reach the end of the valley by nightfall. If my directions are correct, one day's march should bring us to one of your outlying towns. From there, we can rent a carriage to take us to your palace. Home within three days, Paul."

Paul had spent twelve days tramping across Nivram earlier that month and was not looking forward to a further two. "More walking," he muttered. "Once I'm back in the palace, I shall never walk again."

Tremere bent down, picked up a handful of dirt, and let it fall through his fingers. "What happened here?"

"Queen Rose's floating castle was here," Paul said. "It must have scorched the land when it left." Bad enough that the evil Queen Rose had selected his country to stay in. Worse was the destruction of the valley that she left behind.

"I have a bad feeling about this place," Tremere said, shaking his head.

Paul did too. He glanced up at the sky where a solitary dark cloud hovered high above their heads, and then at the narrow sides of the valley, veiled in shadow. He couldn't shake the sensation of being watched. The burnt earth appeared soft and yielding, as if ready to swallow anyone who stepped on it. A faint acrid smell drifted on the breeze and he wrinkled his nose in disgust.

"We should avoid the bog and walk along its perimeter," Tremere said.

The blackened earth stretched from one side of the valley to the other, leaving only a narrow gap between its edge and the mountainside.

"If you want." Paul did not relish lingering there a moment longer than necessary.

As they walked, Tremere asked Paul about his home. Paul suspected it was to distract his thoughts from any possible danger, but he never minded talking about the palace.

"The palace is beautiful," he began. "It is very old, built by my great-great-great – well, I am not quite sure how many greats, but it is ancient, and made of pure white marble. My private quarters are spacious, and I command the best views over the city. Naturally I spend time with various tutors to learn all the noble arts: fencing, archery, strategy, politics, history and so forth." Paul paused. It seemed a long time since he had received any schooling, and it was quite an effort to recall his subjects. "Astronomy. Ethics and logic. Em, philosophy..."

"Sounds a lot of work." Tremere sounded amused.

Paul bristled a little. "For other people maybe. For the royal prince and heir..." He stopped. He sounded just like Frolley, one of his tutors, only not as dry and sarcastic. "I study drama as well," he added lamely. "I like drama."

"Who else lives in the palace?"

"My regent, Reece, who has looked after my country since I was a baby. I won't inherit the throne until I reach twenty-five. There are many servants, naturally. My own personal ones and many general purpose ones." Numerous servants milled about the palace but Paul was unaware of what they all did. "And guards, lots of palace guards. They parade around the battlements and look magnificent."

"What are the people like? Are they happy? Do they live in prosperity or poverty?"

"The people are noble and brave," Paul said warmly. "They are incredibly loyal and devoted to their royal house. They would die for me." Tremere shot him a quick glance over his shoulder. Paul read disbelief into it. "It's true." He had been taught this all his life.

"I did not doubt you. I only wonder why you have so many palace guards if your people are so devoted."

Paul knew the answer to this one. "They are a passionate and fiery race, but alas too easily led. I must be a strong leader so that they will not raise an arm against me." He sighed as he finished. Fourteen years earlier his father had been murdered by a rabble that had broken into the palace when he was a baby. His father, he understood, had been too soft. He had given the people freedom and they had reciprocated by killing him.

The travellers reached the far side of the valley. Sheer cliffs of grey rock reared above their heads, but higher up crumbling ledges broke the rock face. Tremere stared at them as if he feared enemies were perched there out of sight.

"Strength is not only, or always, measured by force," Tremere said. "But let us go quietly now."

A pebble rolled down the cliff. As it fell, it gathered up other pieces of grit until a shower fell on top of the travellers. Paul spluttered, and brushed the dust out of his eyes.

"Let's move," Tremere whispered.

The dark blemish on the valley floor stretched its fingers, occasionally touching the rocky walls, but for the most part there was a clear path wide enough for them to follow. Paul kept close to the cliff and walked as quickly as he could after Tremere, stepping over any tendrils of black earth that crossed the way.

The smell grew stronger, an unpleasant burnt stench. Little landslides of dirt and grit dribbled down the walls, as if someone was mimicking their journey above their heads. Paul glanced up occasionally but saw nothing.

On his right, the black stained earth trembled and a ripple surged across it.

"Hurry, Tremere," Paul said, gripped by a feeling the bog was alive and wanted to eat him.

Tremere broke into a run, Paul pounded at his heels.

Ahead a large part of the black bog completely covered their path.

"Can you leap across?" Tremere demanded.

Paul didn't hesitate. "Yes, yes, go on," he urged. He heard rock grating above his head, and more small stones rained about him.

Tremere sprang across the bog. As Paul jumped in turn, he realised that he would not, *could not*, make it. His feet landed in the bog. Before he could shout out, Tremere seized his arm. By then, he was already up to his waist in the mire, and sinking rapidly. Tremere strained to yank him clear of the bog and onto the stony earth beyond it.

Paul lay there gasping, covered to his chest in muck from the swamp. It reeked, and Paul's vision of returning triumphantly to the land of his birth finally died. After all the work the Milkens had spent cleaning his gear and restoring it to pristine condition, his clothes were ruined once again.

Tremere leaned over him, a look of concern on his face. "Are you all right?"

Paul nodded and dragged himself to his feet, wondering how best he could slip into the palace without anyone seeing him.

"We should continue," Tremere said in a low voice. "Once we are clear of this foul bog, we can rest a while."

"Very well." Paul tried to summon a more dignified manner than his appearance entailed. "I am ready to go on."

It was a relief to leave the black bog behind. The valley sloped treacherously, its surface uneven and strewn with rocks. They had to pick their way carefully.

The sun was low in the sky when Tremere and Paul reached the end of the valley. A panoply of reds, pinks, and oranges spread across the horizon, but for the travellers in the valley all was gloom. Trees loomed ahead, their roots tangled in undergrowth.

They stopped for the night in a small clearing. Paul warmed his hands at the small fire Tremere built. The mossy earth was soft and thick with pine needles. Some of these Tremere tossed into the blaze. The strong scent of pine pleasantly obscured the stink of bog dirt hardened into his clothes. In two days he would be home. Maybe Tremere could purchase him a cloak to cover his filthy apparel?

Paul took a drink from his water bottle, tightened the cap to prevent any spillage, and lay back on his blanket.

Above, branches danced together in a light breeze, and through their tangled arms he could make out the night sky. Cathy was always going on about the stars. Although Paul had studied astronomy for several years and could name every star that blazed in the heavens, he could not remember gazing admiringly at them.

Until now, when it struck him as a beautiful spectacle. He made a mental note to visit the palace observatory.

Weary limbs combined with fresh air allowed sleep to quickly overtake him. He woke with a startled exclamation to a hand grabbing his shoulder.

"What?" he stammered, blinking the sleep from his eyes. Night still embraced the trees, and only the dying embers of the fire remained to disturb the darkness. Half a dozen figures, blacker than the wood, surrounded him. Tremere lay slumped on the ground, dead or unconscious. A rough arm dragged Paul to his feet and held him in an iron grip.

Shock gripped Paul. Why would anyone molest him in this manner? He was their beloved prince and future ruler. Some of his captors exchanged a few words, too low for Paul to catch. A muffled groan caught his attention, and he saw Tremere stir on the ground. He was glad that Tremere was alive, but what a terrible way to treat his friend, and guest of the country. These rebels would pay dearly for their actions.

Tremere rose and staggered against one of the men, but the rebels were ready and Tremere was knocked back to the ground. When they dragged him to his feet again, Paul caught the glint of a knife placed against Tremere's throat.

A voice snarled. "Be very careful. I've no reason to keep you alive, mate."

Paul recognised the accent as that of the capital city. As the man held up the knife, his cloak fell back to reveal a sleeve and jacket that was all too familiar to Paul. *It was that of his personal guard.*

Why had his palace guard turned against him? Had there been a rebellion during his three-month absence? But then fury overcame his shock, and he found his voice.

"Release me! At once!" he demanded. "My friend too. How *dare* you touch me!"

His captors ignored him and Paul, fuming, was half-dragged through the trees.

Another clearing appeared ahead. Lanterns raised on poles illuminated a large company of soldiers gathered in orderly formation. The pain of seeing his suspicions confirmed was enough to make Paul wish Lucky had never rescued him.

A slim figure, clad in soldiers' garb, stood waiting to receive them. Tremere was flung to the ground and rolled onto his back, and a foot placed on his chest. Paul was allowed to remain standing.

"Well, well, what have we here?" The voice was cool, faintly amused. "Another filthy rebel cornered in its lair. Well done, men. The citizens of this great country can sleep a little easier tonight."

The figure bent a little and leaned over to stare at Tremere's face. They pushed back their visor and then removed the whole helmet. Long fair hair, gleaming silver in the starlight, fell around a face that was pale and cold.

"Your face is not at all evil. Your kind are learning to hide their intentions better. All the same, it will serve as a warning to others once it is parted from your shoulders," she said.

Tremere made no movement nor gave any sign that he heard a word addressed to him, but Paul spluttered in anger.

"Reece! What are you doing? Why did you attack us?"

The soldier turned away from Tremere and looked at Paul.

"It's good to have you back, your majesty," Reece said. "Don't worry. We'll make sure this villain is properly punished." She made a sign and the men grasping Paul immediately let him go and stood back.

"Reece," Paul tried to compose himself and speak calmly. "Reece, release my friend."

"It's for your own protection," she said. She called over one of her men. "Look after the prince."

Before he knew what was happening, Paul was dragged away to be cleaned up and escorted to the palace, leaving the regent and most of her soldiers in the clearing with Tremere.

"Reece," Paul shouted but she had turned away and appeared not to hear him.

Chapter Six

UNDERGROUND

V icky blinked into consciousness. The darkness was so
complete she panicked until she remembered the plunge
into the pit. She shuddered, recalling how far she had fallen
before the sphere hit the ground and shattered. She must have
hit her head. It still throbbed, and when she touched her
forehead, her fingers came away sticky. She tried moving but her
limbs felt bruised and battered. It was amazing she hadn't been
smashed to pieces.

"Ouch!" She wouldn't move so quickly again.

She felt about for her telescope, and her fingers touched
smooth metal. Immediately it glowed, as if her touch activated
it. Vicky snatched it up and held it close. By the telescope's
silvery sheen, Vicky could see she was in a large, circular pit,
whose smooth clay sides disappeared into darkness above her
head. Too sore to move, she shut her eyes. *Only for a few
moments rest...*

When she woke next, it felt like hours had passed. Her body was still stiff and bruised, but her head had cleared. *Susan*! She was on a rescue mission, and instead of finding Susan, she had spent the time having a nice nap.

Annoyed with herself, she got to her feet. The telescope cast enough light to show large rubbery shards scattered about. The sphere must have cushioned her fall. It was impossible to see how far the walls of the pit rose, but she was certain she was a long way below the surface of the earth. A narrow tunnel led away from the shaft. A faint draft came from its direction. Susan must have been taken that way, for there was no other exit.

The ceiling of the passageway was low and its floor uneven. Holding the telescope before her, Vicky stooped to enter the tunnel, grateful that she wasn't claustrophobic. The passage twisted and turned, and soon her back ached, a nagging thirst plagued her, and she was besieged by doubts. She'd never find her way back. Hopelessly lost underground, she was doomed never to see the sky again. Susan's sphere most likely fell down some other pit. No one would ever discover what happened to either of them...Vicky gritted her teeth and tried to ignore the voice that told her she was making yet another mistake.

After some time, the tunnel made a sharp turn right and began to descend. Vicky didn't need the glimmer of her telescope any more. Something ahead glowed a warm red, reflecting light through the tunnel, and soon the passage ended in an enormous cavern.

Vicky, relieved to be able to straighten, exited onto a wide rocky ledge near the cavern roof. A stone balustrade protected the edge and she was able to duck behind this to peep out at what lay below.

A blast of heat struck her face and a plume of smoke made her eyes smart. A huge fire burned in the centre of the cavern. Several figures huddled near the fire. Vicky gasped. Above the shimmering green cloaks they wore, she saw knobbly hairless skulls, scaly skin, long snout-like noses, and oval yellow eyes. Three-toed feet, claw-like and unshod, peeped beneath the hem of their cloaks. She couldn't see any tails, but they reminded her of two legged lizards. Extremely tall lizards, for she guessed they'd reach her shoulder.

They must be after Susan's flute all the same. Vicky made sure her telescope was back in its pouch so they wouldn't glimpse it.

One of them moved closer to the fire and rubbed his scaly claws together. He said something to his companion, which Vicky couldn't catch.

On thinking back, Vicky was sure the amount of shards clearly showed two spheres had broken into pieces. Which meant these creatures had passed here earlier with Susan, so there had to be a way down to the cavern floor. Vicky crawled along beside the parapet.

At the end of the ledge a thick rope, knotted at intervals, snaked its way to the cavern floor. Vicky was a good climber, and the knots made it look easy. She gave it an experimental tug. The rope seemed firmly attached to the rock by a large iron staple. She hoped nobody had seen her shake the rope.

She peered over the balustrade again.

Nobody was in sight. The guards must have gone. The fire roared on, unattended. Vicky decided to risk the rope. Her skirt had torn during her fall, and she increased the tear to enable her to descend by the rope. Luckily she had worn her leggings underneath.

The knots proved to be good footholds, and Vicky quickly shimmied down. The floor of the cavern was black rock, hard and uneven, but before she could take a step, a voice spoke behind her.

"Do not move."

There hadn't been anybody there a moment ago. Vicky whirled about. Still nobody there.

"Remain where you are," a second voice said.

Scared, Vicky hit out in panic with her telescope. She heard a cry and the sound of tearing as the telescope made contact with something, and then one of the guards appeared in front of her. His green cloak was torn, and he gazed in horror at the ripped material.

"You've ruined it," the creature croaked.

Vicky did not stop to discuss the matter. Pushing hard at the creature she *could* see, she ran for an exit into a wide, well-lit tunnel.

A whistle went up behind her.

Vicky didn't know what it meant, and kept going until three small figures appeared ahead, blocking the passageway.

All three held long blades that shone in the torchlight. Vicky skidded to a halt. Then she felt the cold prick of steel on her neck and she knew she was surrounded.

"All right, you got me," she said, raising her hands and trying to stop them shaking. "So tell me where Susan is?"

The air shimmered. Another twenty of the green-cloaked figures appeared. Vicky gulped. She had been that close to fighting, thinking she only had three opponents. She couldn't do anything against so many. Why hadn't she gone back for Lucky? How did she imagine she could do anything to help Susan? Now *nobody* knew where Susan was.

She'd probably die at the hands of these strange creatures, furlongs below earth, and nobody would ever learn what had become of her.

Serve you right for being so stupid, she thought.

"Walk," a harsh voice behind her said, and a claw pressed against her back.

Vicky reluctantly took a step forward.

"I need to know what you've done with my sister," Vicky said, the telescope hanging around her neck giving her courage. "Why did you kidnap her? What do you want with her?"

Her captors remained silent, urging her on by the blade at her throat and the claw on her back.

"Who are you?"

The steel pressed a little harder and Vicky understood that she was not to ask anything further. She fell silent, afraid the guard would use the knife to cut her throat.

She was marched towards a tunnel which intersected the passage, and a short distance along this tunnel she reached a door cut into the rock with neither handle nor lock. One of the creatures made some kind of hand signal and the door slid open. Vicky was shoved in, the door shut behind her.

The cave was small, lit by a single torch which burned brightly on the wall, and contained a table, a chair, and a mattress.

Curled up on the mattress lay Susan, her right arm in a sling. Vicky dropped by Susan's side and gently touched her shoulder to wake her.

"Vicky?" Susan blinked a few times as if she thought she was dreaming. "What are you doing here?"

"What happened to your arm?" Vicky said, her relief at finding her sister tempered by concern for her injury.

"Oh, I fell climbing down that rope. I think it's sprained. They bandaged it for me." Susan sat up, wincing a little. "How did you find me? Is Lucky here?"

"Em, no." Vicky forced a bright smile. "I came to rescue you myself."

Susan looked disappointed but quickly smiled. "I'm glad you're here." She scooted up on the mattress to make room for Vicky.

Vicky's eye fell on a pitcher on the ground beside Susan. "Is that water?"

Susan passed the jug to her. "It's drinkable."

Vicky's mouth was so dry she would have drunk anything. The contents of the jug seemed sweet and refreshing and she drank most of it.

"Food too." Susan passed a golden plate with some kind of bread.

Tough and chewy though it was, the peculiar taste didn't stop Vicky from devouring half of it.

"At least they feed their prisoners," she said once she finished. "Why have they kidnapped you? What do they want?"

"I'm afraid they're after my flute," Susan said in a whisper. "They asked me if I had anything that belonged to another and not to me, and I said no. Somebody is going to arrive tomorrow to speak to me about it. I suppose they captured you for your telescope."

"Not quite. I followed you here." Vicky gave her a brief synopsis of her journey. "They have invisible cloaks. Only for my telescope, I'd never have seen where you went. Maybe they were going to come back for me, but I reckon they threw that stuff over me to stop me following them."

"Invisible cloaks." Susan gave a shiver. "They could be here, in this room, listening to us."

Vicky held her telescope to her eye, wishing she had thought of using it back in the cavern.

"Nobody here," she whispered. "But I think you're right, they want the flute. We should hide it."

"But where?" Susan looked miserable. "Under this mattress? There's nowhere else."

"I have an idea." Vicky fiddled with her telescope.

A moment later she removed one end, exposing the hollow centre. She had used the secret cavity before to hide things.

"It won't fit." Susan held up her flute. It was a slim instrument, but so too was Vicky's telescope. In fact, they looked similar in size.

"Let's try it." Vicky took the flute and slotted it neatly inside the tube. "Like it was made for it."

"*Made for it*," Susan repeated. "I wonder if it was."

Vicky replaced the end and held it up to the light.

It looked like a telescope to her, but if, in fact, it was a case for the Lost Flute of Thule... that explained why the Diamonds had never come across it before. Vicky slipped the telescope back in to its pouch, noticing that it weighed no heavier.

"Now we need to plan our escape," she said.

Chapter Seven

ZANIA

C athy woke with a start, for a moment confused about why she was rolled in a blanket and lying on the ground next to the remains of a fire. Then she saw Alan, poking the embers with a stick, and she remembered. A long flight across the patchwork of fields as Mount Slant shrank into the distance. Then came mountains and deep valleys, followed by plains and a fast-flowing river. Finally, as the day melded into dusk, Charlie had stopped for the night.

Cathy sat up. "Where's Charlie?"

"He's gone to spy out the land," Alan said. His charred stick crumbled into ash. "Looking for Nuones."

Cathy pulled her blanket around her shoulders to keep the chill air at bay. Pale gleams of gold spread across the sky, chasing away the night. She clasped her compass tightly, hoping she was brave enough for whatever lay ahead.

A soft *whishing* noise announced Charlie's return. Cathy was impressed with how softly the canoe landed.

"Awake?" Charlie said. "Good. Time to go."

"What about breakfast?" Alan rummaged in his bag.

"Eat on the move," Charlie said.

Cathy yawned as she scrambled to her feet. Alan passed her a couple of bread rolls, which she gratefully accepted. An empty void seemed to exist where her stomach should have been.

"Make sure the fire is out, won't you?" Charlie said, keeping his wooden frame a few feet away.

Alan kicked at the remains of the fire, and it disintegrated into a pile of ash.

"Out. Did you see any Nuones, Charlie?"

"Not one." Charlie looked anxious, as if he regretted undertaking the journey. "We should reach Zania by early afternoon. I have some contacts there who'll arrange a boat for you."

"Aren't you coming with us, Charlie?" Cathy felt a stab of fear that Charlie might not accompany them to Thule.

"I can't," Charlie said simply. "I'd like to, but I can't leave the Diamond realms. Not without permission from the king, which is, I'm afraid, impossible to obtain at the moment."

"Couldn't you get it later? Afterwards, I mean." Alan said.

Cathy bit her lip. "Lucky wouldn't want you to leave us."

"I know. But you'll be leaving me this time," Charlie said. "Follow the compass, Cathy."

Cathy pulled at her silver chain and stared at the little dial that hung at the end of it.

"Due east," she said, disappointed it wasn't pointing west to Mount Slant. She didn't want to go to Thule without Charlie.

"Hop aboard," Charlie called cheerily. "Zania lies in the path of the sun."

The red-gold orb of the sun appeared over the horizon, and the sky was filled with liquid gold as Charlie took to the skies once more. Blinded by the rising sun, Cathy had to face west and watch the shadows recede from the land as the sun rose in all its glory.

She lay low in Charlie's snug, padded interior, sheltered from the breeze, occasionally peering out at the countryside below. The morning passed before she saw that fertile fields had replaced the barren mountainous land. In the distance, a shimmering blue curve announced the sea. She sat low out of the slipstream and unscrewed the cap of her water bottle. Hours of flight left her thirsty. Shortly after this, and less gracefully than earlier, Charlie landed with a thump on some grass.

"Sorry, harder to resist gravity when you're tired," he said.

Alan woke with a start. "Where's Zania?"

"A short walk away," the canoe said. "Better not to fly in. I don't want to frighten the residents."

Cathy climbed out of the canoe and stretched. "Thanks for flying us here, Charlie." She stole a glance at her compass. No change. Charlie was following the correct path.

Charlie had landed by a low wall, on the other side of which animals grazed. Some looked over and lowed at the strangers.

"Aren't they pretty?" Cathy said. She had never seen them before. "What lovely brown eyes they have."

"Cows, are they?" Alan stared at them.

"Yes, but bulls this side of the wall," Charlie said. "Come on."

Cathy hadn't noticed two large animals watching them from a nearby knoll. Their leather skins were black, horns protruded from their skulls, and there was a distinctly unfriendly gleam in their eyes. One of them lowered his head and gave a bellow.

"Charlie," Cathy said nervously. The bulls looked scary.

"This way." Alan ran towards a wooden gate.

Cathy turned to follow but slipped in some dirt and fell flat on her face. As she pushed herself up, she noticed three things all at once. First, there was no sign of the canoe. Secondly, Alan had reached the gate but looked back with an expression of horror. Thirdly, the bull was almost on top of her, its massive horns, sharpened to a point, bearing down, about to spear her. Cathy screwed her eyes shut, waiting to be torn in two and tossed halfway across the field. She felt the bull's breath in her face and then nothing.

"Hurry, I can't hold them long," Charlie gasped.

Cathy opened her eyes. Less than half an inch above her stomach, two black horns gleamed wickedly in the sunlight, but came no closer.

Cathy wriggled out from under the bull, jumped to her feet and ran. She flung herself at the gate and Alan grabbed her arm to help her over. At the top she stopped to look back. The second bull had paused several feet behind the first, tail up and hoof raised. Then, the moment fracturing, the first bull's horns dug into the earth, and the second animal pulled himself short of the ditch with a roar of rage. Cathy dropped down on to a laneway and glanced at Charlie, now in Diamond form, perched on the top bar. "Thanks."

"Nothing to thank me for," Charlie said. "I landed you there in the first place." A flash of light and he was sitting on her shoulder. "Who'd have thought they could move so fast?"

Cathy brushed mud from her hands and walked along the lane beside Alan. The laneway led to a wider road. Charlie directed them right, and soon the hedges on the seaward side disappeared and the roadway faded into a grassy track before all trace of it was obliterated. Cathy inhaled the salty sea air and heard the gulls mournfully crying out as they flew overhead.

Rather than gently tapering to the sea, as Cathy expected, the land ended abruptly. A profusion of colourful flowers grew along the cliff edge. Shrubs and dwarf trees adorned low white walls, and stone benches were dotted among them. It looked a delightful place to sit out and gaze towards the sea. Then Cathy noticed small white stone blocks and realised she was looking at a graveyard. A paved pathway wound its way among the headstones.

"Follow the path to the cliff," Charlie said.

The burial ground stretched along the cliff top in both directions but was itself quite narrow so it took no time to cross it. From the cliff edge, Cathy looked down on a curved golden beach, sparkling blue sea, and a line of white houses huddled against the base of the chalk cliff. The only way down to the beach was a precipitous path cut into the cliff face. The steps looked uneven and dangerous.

"Down there?" she faltered.

"There's a handrail," Charlie said. "It's safe."

A rope hung loosely between occasional pitons in the rock.

Cathy didn't want to contradict him but it struck her as anything but safe.

"Looks easy," Alan said. He never felt the slightest fear of heights. He probably wouldn't even use the rope, Cathy thought enviously.

Alan led the way, and she waited until he was five stairs down before she followed. She tried not to look at the dizzying drop to the dazzling white rooftops below. Little walkways cut away from the flight of steps, leading to openings in the chalky cliff. Some were large, six foot in height and almost as broad. Others were small and round, set into the rock like windows with ledges as windowsills. Some ledges had boxes of flowers, blue and pink geraniums, while others had miniature herb gardens. Steps had been cut into the cliff in places to allow access between two caverns, one above the other, as if they were two storey homes. Some entrances had colourful flowers growing out of the rock, and outside others strings of washing were hung.

Nearby, a woman was singing as she strung an armful of colourful clothes across a washing line between two of the cliff caves. Cathy noticed large baskets fixed to some kind of pulley system farther along the cliff. What a strange place to live, she thought, like nesting birds in the cliff.

She was glad to finally reach the ground. A short sandy lane flanked on either side by squat, white buildings led to a main street that ran the width of the bay, separating the houses from the shore. The sea was a deep blue and birds bobbed in the water. Farther out, Cathy could see several fishing boats, and beyond them nothing but sea stretching to infinity.

Next stop Thule.

Chapter Eight

THE FIREBIRD

S usan was happy to have Vicky's company but she wished her younger sister had gone to Lucky for help. Being captured by a giant sphere, rolled across the hills and dropped down a deep pit had been a terrifying experience, and her only hope had been that Vicky had rushed off to tell Lucky.

She told herself that perhaps the strange lizard-like creatures weren't so bad. After all, they had bandaged her wrist and brought her food, little hard biscuits that were quite tasty, and a jug of water. She had got used to their liquid ochre eyes and their scaly snouts and the strange little bumps that covered their heads. But when she saw how roughly they shoved Vicky into the cell she changed her mind.

It looked like Lucky wouldn't be coming to rescue them so it was up to them to escape. The only exit from the cell was by the door which seemed to be part of the wall. No amount of kicking or shoving by Vicky made a dent in it. Vicky even tried hitting it with her telescope (Susan couldn't watch) before she flung herself on the mattress beside Susan and fumed silently.

"It's all right, Vicky," Susan said, giving her a quick hug. "We'll find a way, and if not, Lucky will soon turn up."

"Why don't you play your flute and hypnotise the guards to let us out?" Vicky sat up as if struck by genius.

"I don't know how to do that," Susan said frankly. The flute played whatever tune it wished, and if that was to heal a wound or lull someone to sleep, it was beyond Susan's control.

"Let's attack the guards the next time they come into the cell," Vicky said eagerly. "You distract them and I'll hit them with my telescope."

"How will we get out of the tunnels? I couldn't climb that rope one-handed, and even if I could, I'd never scale that pit, could you?"

Vicky was not so easily put off. "Those creatures got out and kidnapped you, there *must* be a way."

Susan wasn't so sure. She imagined the guards scuttling up the sides of the pit, using all four limbs, but she agreed to Vicky's plan. They had to do something.

The only problem was the guards didn't return. Vicky yelled until she was hoarse but nobody came. Eventually she curled up beside Susan on the mattress and fell asleep.

It didn't take long for Susan to fall into a dreamless sleep and she woke to a hand on her shoulder. Vicky's anxious face looked down at her.

"I heard something, I think the guards are coming," she said eagerly. "This is our chance."

Susan struggled to her feet as the cell door slid open and a dozen guards piled in.

They didn't seem so kindly with swords in their claws.

Vicky made a dash for the exit but one of the guards caught her by her plait, two more seized her arms while a fourth pointed his sword to Vicky's heart.

Susan shrieked and flung herself at them, but two of the guards grabbed her and held her.

Another one said something but Susan could not understand it. From the impatient movement of his claw, she guessed she was meant to follow. While she hesitated, one of them touched her arm. She shook off the claw and stalked out of the cell.

Susan lost count of the series of tunnels she was led through until the guards finally reached a small low-ceilinged chamber and Susan was pushed forward.

The cavern was empty apart from two more of the strange creatures. One held his green cloak closely about him, but the garment worn by the other was golden and fastened at the shoulder. A golden circlet crowned his head.

She heard him speak but his words were unintelligible. When Susan looked blankly at him, he muttered something, waved and spoke again. This time she understood.

"I am Sylverine, leader of the Nuones. You have something that belongs to another."

"No, I don't." Something about him intimidated her, but she managed to squeeze out an answer.

He stared hard at her. "Where is it?"

"I don't know what you are talking about," she said, stepping back from him but bumping into another guard.

He turned to his companion. "Haspin."

Haspin stepped forward. His colouring was lighter and he seemed a little taller but otherwise he bore a striking resemblance to Sylverine. From beneath his green cloak he withdrew a small lantern and held it in front of Susan.

A thin trail of green smoke issued from it as he waved it slowly from side to side.

"This is the fire of Thule. By its flame, you shall heed my words. What is your name?"

Susan gazed fascinated at it. "Susan." She didn't want to reply but somehow her lips moved and words tumbled out.

"Do you have the flute?"

"What flute?" Susan wasn't going to lie but she was equally determined not to reveal its whereabouts, no matter how much the magical smoke made her want to.

A faint acrid smell rose from the smoke. "The flute of Thule, given to Scatherina many years ago."

"No."

"Did you ever have it?"

"Yes."

"Do you know where it is now?"

"No." She did not know *exactly* where it was.

Haspin lowered the lantern. "She speaks the truth. Are you sure you took the right child?"

Sylverine rubbed his scaly chin. "She admitted she had it. Ask her where she left it."

"I didn't leave it anywhere," Susan said, her voice trembling with the effort to keep herself from telling where the flute was hidden. "Dulstar wanted to study it and I said he could and Lucky said it would be safe..." Her voice tailed off.

"The Diamonds have it," Sylverine said slowly. "*She* won't be pleased to hear that."

"Search the girl," Haspin said sharply.

Susan squawked as one of the guards quickly patted her down and shook his head.

"Take her away," Haspin said. "She can feed the fire of the east chamber."

"What?" Susan was startled. She didn't want to feed any fire. "Can't I go home now? I don't have what you want..."

Haspin fixed her with a mesmerising stare.

"You shall be released in three days, as long as you assist in our tasks, and make no attempt to escape. We can lock you up forever if you prefer."

"Nnno," Susan said. "What about Vicky?"

"She will be treated the same."

Before Susan could say any more, she was bundled out of the chamber, past Vicky who was surrounded by guards, and down more corridors to a large chamber. It looked similar to the one where she had sprained her wrist, except there was no rope to the upper balcony. A huge fire burned in a great golden bowl. The guard showed her how to shovel clods of dark earth into a chute which fed the fire.

"I am Roche," the Nuone guard told her. "Do it like this."

It was awkward with one hand but soon Susan got the hang of it. The guard sat on a stool to watch her, wrapped its cloak around itself and vanished.

Susan didn't think that was fair. Now she wouldn't know if he was there or not. Glancing over occasionally towards the seat, she ploughed on as best she could.

After a few minutes, she spoke. "Roche?"

A moment's silence. Then a green shimmer and Roche appeared. "Yes?"

He, or she, seemed quite nice, even a little unsure of his role as guard.

"What is your job here?"

"Secret Nuone stuff," Roche replied. "No more talking, please." He disappeared once more.

Susan returned to her shovelling and worked in silence for a while. Something ached inside her and she realised it was the loss of her flute paining her. She tried not to think about it and focused on shovelling . It was warm work, and she quickly grew thirsty.

A goblet and jug of water had been left on a ledge. With only one good hand, it was awkward to fill. As she took a sip of water, a noise caught her ear. It was sweet and musical but stopped almost immediately.

Susan trembled at the thought they had discovered the telescope's hiding place and were now playing her flute.

Sad, mournful strains echoed through the tunnels. The flute could play every emotion, even the heart-breaking loneliness that she now heard, but something told her that whatever made the sound, it was not her flute.

Close by, somebody was lonely and in trouble.

She paused in her work. After a few moments she heard the sorrowful cry once more echo through the tunnels.

"What was that, Roche?" she asked.

No answer from the guard. Was he still there or had he slipped away?

The keening sound came again. Susan felt drawn to investigate. She put down the shovel.

"I'll be back shortly," she said.

Susan stepped as quietly as she could along the tunnel that led to her cell. The cry came again, sweet yet melancholic. She put a hand on one of the golden walls and felt it throb. The cry drew her on past her own cell to a small door with a visible bolt. She took a deep breath, slipped back the bolt, opened the door, and stepped inside, pulling the door shut behind her.

A blast of heat met Susan but she didn't heed it. Her eyes were drawn first to a huge nest of soft white feathers heaped on one side of the chamber. An enormous cauldron of some blue liquid was placed directly opposite, but huddled between the two was the strangest creature Susan had ever seen.

Enormous blue eyes, flecked with shards of gold, were set in a head shaped rather like a horse. Its long neck curved gracefully down to a round body, folded wings, and four strong legs ending in talon-like feet. Susan glimpsed the beginnings of a tail, but the creature seemed to be sitting on it. The most unusual thing was that the creature was covered with long red plumes, and beneath the feathers Susan thought she could distinguish a golden skin.

At her entrance the creature moved nervously back against the wall.

"It's all right," Susan said, trying to soothe it. She wasn't sure if it was a horse or a bird or some strange combination, but it looked gentle. She moved towards it.

In response the creature opened its mouth. Flame shot out as it emitted a pitying cry.

Susan jumped back, fell into the downy nest, and for a moment choked on the feathers as she struggled to sit up. The creature backed itself as far away from her as possible, into the opposite part of the cave.

It was frightened of *her*.

A wave of sympathy for the creature spread through Susan at this realisation, giving her the courage to scramble to her feet and jump out of the nest.

"It's all right," she cooed. "It's all right." She held her hands out to show that she meant no harm. "You're a firebird, aren't you?"

She didn't know where the name came from. It popped into her head from nowhere. A fire-breathing four-legged bird.

The creature still trembled violently but at least it did not breathe any more flame. Susan stayed where she was and continued talking.

"My name is Susan. I'm a friend of Lucky the Diamond. I've been taken here by the Nuones. I'm a prisoner too, like you." She noticed golden chains manacled to the firebird's feet. "I have to go now before they miss me, but I will be back. Perhaps we can help each other."

The firebird looked at her as if it understood, though still it trembled. Susan made her farewells and slipped back to the chamber with the fire.

"Roche?" she called quietly.

There was no reply. Sighing with relief, she resumed her duties.

After a little while, the keening began again. The sorrowful notes almost broke Susan's heart. She longed to return to the firebird's side, but it was too soon to slip away again. She was afraid that Roche was really present, trying to trick her.

Roche appeared sometime later with more hard biscuits and another flagon of water. He told her that Vicky was working in a different chamber and that Susan would see her soon.

"You must work now," he said. "The fire burns low."

As far as Susan could tell, the fire burned hotter than ever, but she resumed shovelling.

Roche disappeared every few hours, and Susan took the opportunity to visit the firebird again. Each time, the firebird looked less frightened, and when Susan returned to work, there were longer gaps between cries.

Eventually Roche said work was over and led her back to her cell.

"Sleep now," he said. "Duties will resume in the morning."

"Where's Vicky?" Susan said crossly.

"The other prisoner works in another chamber. You will see her soon." With that Roche slid the prison door shut.

Her limbs ached from tending the fire, and she was badly bruised from her earlier fall down the pit, so Susan gladly fell onto the couch in her cell. Anxious as she was about her sister, Susan still fell asleep easily and dreamed of the firebird, its keening reverberating through her dreams.

Strangely the pain caused by the loss of her flute had been eased.

Chapter Nine

VICKY IS SET TO WORK

When Vicky was bundled into the presence of the leader of the Nuones, she was partly angry at being held prisoner, slightly relieved at seeing Susan looking unharmed, but mostly terrified. Scared her captors would find Susan's flute, she was also petrified by whatever plans they had. They had taken Susan for a reason, but Vicky just invited herself along. Maybe they would decide the best thing was to get rid of her? Her first glance at the golden-cloaked Nuone and his green-cloaked companion convinced her that was their intention.

She wasn't going to make it easy for them so she stuck her chin up and glared at her captors as if she wasn't trembling like a jelly on the inside.

"You better release us," she said immediately. "Before Lucky hears of this."

"I am Sylverine, leader of the Nuones," the Nuone clad in the golden cloak said. "You speak our language well."

"You speak my language well too," Vicky retorted. "We're friends of Lucky, so I'd advise you to let us go free."

Lucky's name didn't have the effect Vicky had expected.

"I do not know anyone of that name. I will ask you only once. What are you doing here?"

"I'm here for Susan, my sister. You kidnapped her. And Lucky is the daughter of the King of the Diamonds. Don't tell me you don't know who the Diamonds are."

"They will not bother us. What have you about your neck?"

His sharp eyes had spotted her pouch. Vicky called herself a lot of names for not concealing it better beneath her tunic. Before she could reply, his claw had shot out and removed her telescope.

Vicky instinctively flung herself at him but she was held back by the guards, and seethed as Sylverine tipped her treasure out of the pouch and held it up. The telescope shone in his claw. Vicky could scarcely breathe.

"What is it?" Sylverine said.

"My telescope." Her hands tightened into fists. She'd have to snatch it back and make a run for it.

Sylverine held the tube up to one eye. Vicky's wonderfully clever plan was falling apart. Now the creature was going to get *both* her telescope and Susan's flute.

But Sylverine lowered his arm and handed the telescope to his companion. "Take it, Haspin."

Vicky let out a long breath. Sylverine hadn't noticed the flute. The other creature showed no interest in it either, merely slipping it beneath his cloak. "That is *my* telescope. I want it back," she said.

Sylverine muttered something that Vicky couldn't make out.

"We shall return it later," he said, waving a claw. "In your species, what is the most important quality?"

The conversation had taken a strange turn.

"Em…" Vicky didn't know what to answer. In Lowdar, money, success, possessions and status were deemed important. But now it seemed to her that friendship and loyalty mattered more. Courage too. She knew Diamonds like Lucky and Charlie believed in a whole lot of other things, like being fair, even to evil monsters like Queen Rose, and in truth, even if it hurt.

Sylverine's question appeared to have been rhetorical.

"Honour. Honour to us is the most important of the virtues. Do you know what honour is?"

"Yeah. Keeping your word. Doing the right thing."

"Can you keep your word, Vicky?" He looked intently at her, his eyes intense and almost mesmerising.

Vicky didn't know if she could. "If I want to," she said.

"I could lock you up in a small dark prison until our work here is done. Or I could allow you some freedom if you give your word to neither interfere with our work nor attempt to flee. Which will it be?"

"I want my telescope back, and I want to go home. With my sister," Vicky said firmly. She wasn't going anywhere without Susan or her telescope.

"In three days you shall. Give me your word."

Three days was a long time. Surely before then, Lucky would have come to their rescue. She knew she couldn't escape the way she had arrived, but maybe there was another way out of the tunnels.

She crossed her fingers behind her back. How she could not escape if an opportunity presented itself?

"All right." It would be worse to be locked up for three days.

"Swear by your telescope and your sister that you will keep your word."

I'm not going to do that, Vicky thought. But with Sylverine's intense eyes upon her, she found herself repeating: "I swear by my sister and upon my telescope that I will not try to escape from this place nor will I hinder your people in their work." Afterwards she wasn't sure how it happened.

"I give you my word that you shall be free to go after three full days," Sylverine pronounced solemnly. "In the meantime, we require your assistance. In exchange, we will procure food and water for you."

Vicky didn't think she should bargain for food. "The least you could do while holding us here is to feed us."

Sylverine said nothing, his silence clearly saying he could do what he wished. It seemed she had no choice.

"Could I have some water now?" The dry thirst returned to tickle her throat once more.

Sylverine made a sign and few moments later, water was presented in an ornate golden flagon. Heavy too, she noticed, as she raised it to her lips. The water was warm but drinkable. She drank so quickly that she spilled some, which trickled down her chin.

Sylverine and his companion stepped away from her but Vicky could clearly hear their discussion.

"Continue the search for the flute, Haspin," Sylverine said. "I promised we'd retrieve it."

"We don't need it for our purposes this time," Haspin snapped. "Waste no more time on it."

"I gave my word," Sylverine said.

A moment's silence ensued.

"I must get back," Sylverine said. "I shall be missed. Until new moon."

"Until new moon." Haspin thumped his tail in farewell as Sylverine slipped into the shadows. Then he turned to Vicky's guards. "Take the prisoner to the west chamber. Keep the two apart."

After she had drunk her fill and eaten most of the plate of cakes the guards had brought her, Vicky was led away through another tunnel. Torches flared at frequent intervals along the walls, bathing the tunnel with golden light. They passed exits to narrower, poorly lit passageways. Eventually the tunnel ended in the same chamber where she had been caught.

The knotted rope had been removed and Vicky knew there was no way she could ascend the smooth side of the chamber without its help. It didn't matter. As Susan said, they'd never be able to climb the pit to the surface. There had to be another way out.

Two guards were on duty. One of them stepped forward and looked at Vicky in what she thought was an unfriendly manner. Perhaps his torn cloak accounted for it.

"I am Otterbek of the Nuones. I will show you how to feed the fire."

The second guard nodded to the first, and left with the creatures who had escorted Vicky to the chamber.

Vicky stared at what looked like a giant bucket full of feathers, a large pail of clods of earth, a pulley system and a chute.

"I'm Vicky," she said in what she hoped was an appeasing manner.

Chapter Ten

LEAVING THE DIAMOND REALM

Zania was a sleepy hamlet of white-washed houses baking in the sun. The houses backed up against the cliff, the flat roofs held benches and planters full of flowers, but nobody was in sight. Temperatures had climbed high and the sea shimmered in the sun. Perhaps in Zania everyone stayed inside in the afternoon.

Alan, wiping the perspiration from his brow, could understand why. However, when they reached the main street, a foot shot out and tripped Alan, and he went sprawling in the dirt.

A shout of laughter greeted his fall, and he peered up to see four boys gathered around.

"What did you do that for?" Cathy cried and pushed the boy who had done it.

The kid looked surprised, but didn't retaliate.

"I'm fine, Cathy." Alan got to his feet and rubbed his hands clean on his trousers. "Why did you trip me?" He kept a wary eye on the largest boy in the group, not because he was the culprit, but from experience he knew always to pick out the biggest opponent.

This boy looked bored.

"Saw you coming down the cliff. You ain't from here, so who are you and what do you want?"

"We're looking for..." Alan stopped. He'd forgotten the names of Charlie's friends.

The four boys closed about the twins.

"Dizzy," Cathy said quickly. "Or Bens. A mutual friend sent us."

The tallest boy frowned.

"Who's the friend?" His voice was laden with suspicion.

"Charlie," Alan said. "Charlie the canoe."

The tall boy's expression changed and he jerked his head at his companions.

"Let 'em go, they're harmless," he said.

"Who's this Charlie, Bens?" the boy who tripped Alan said. "Dunno anyone called that. They're having you on."

"Uncle," Bens said quickly. "I'll take them to my Da. See you lot later." He jerked his head, and the three boys exchanged looks, shrugged, and started to walk away.

Nobody spoke until the three were out of earshot. Then Bens broke the silence.

"What about Charlie? What's the message?"

"He wants to meet you at the far side of the pier," Alan said. Charlie hadn't wanted anyone in Zania to see him in his Diamond form.

Bens looked suspicious. "You lead the way. No tricks."

"Why would we be tricking you?" Cathy began but Alan elbowed her to shut up.

They walked along the sea front, conscious of eyes watching from the row of houses. Cathy kept her head down, but Alan looked around, watching for trouble.

"We're being followed," he said.

Bens glanced back and gave a roar. His three friends ducked away and disappeared among the houses.

At the end of the beach a small pier extended a short way into the sea. On the far side the water was deep enough for a few boats, and Charlie, back in canoe form, was paddling alongside them. He smiled when he saw the twins, accompanied by Bens.

"Hey there," he said. "How have you been, Bens?"

Bens's face lit up. "Hi Charlie! What's going on? Is there trouble? Want my help?"

A grave expression crossed Charlie's face. "Yes, please. I need to borrow a boat, well, my two friends here do. Only for a few days."

Bens said nothing, but Alan noticed the startled look on the boy's face.

"I know," Charlie said. "But I'll explain another time. What about this one here?" He lifted one large foot out of the water and waggled it at a nearby boat.

"No, not that one. It belongs to Harry, and Harry would have my guts for it. You can take our boat," Bens said, pointing to a small red boat at the end of the pier.

"Kind of miniature, isn't it?"

"Fits four." Bens sounded defensive.

"Could you rig up some kind of awning to give them a bit of shelter?" Charlie asked. "They'll be out in the sun for a bit."

"Sure."

"I'll help," Alan said. Boats and the sea fascinated him.

Bens nodded and within a short time, he and Bens had constructed an awning that provided shade to half the boat.

"Where are you going?" Bens said.

"Not sure exactly." Alan didn't think he should share their destination.

Charlie next asked Bens to fill up the twins' water skins, and to spare them a little food.

"We still have some of the supplies that Current gave us," Cathy whispered but Alan nudged her to be quiet. He didn't know how long the food supply was meant to last, and he did not want it to run out prematurely.

Soon the twins were clambering carefully down a short flight of steps and jumping into the boat, which rocked beneath their feet.

"Whoa!" Cathy sat down suddenly.

"You'll have to row clear of the harbour. Are you up to it?" Charlie said.

Alan nodded. He felt up to anything.

"Bring her back in one piece," Bens said. Despite his cheerful tones, he looked nervous. "Otherwise I'm dead."

"Don't worry, we will." Alan sat down and picked up an oar. Cathy sat beside him and took the other. "On three."

Bens untied the mooring rope and threw it in, while Charlie gave them a little nudge to send them off. The twins dug their oars in and a large scoop of water flew into the air and drenched them.

"Sorry," Cathy said, blushing.

"Do it like this," Alan said, demonstrating dipping the oar into the water at an angle. The boat spun clockwise. "Together."

They did not make much progress. Cathy struggled to match Alan's stroke. In the end, Alan took over both oars and pulled strongly. The little boat began to move. Once they had drawn sufficiently distant from the pier, Charlie put out a hand and the boat ploughed through the water.

"I can do it myself," Alan said, raising the oars clear of the water.

"I know, but I don't want you worn out," Charlie replied, spluttering a little as the water ploughed back by the boat hit him in the face.

Charlie pushed the boat until they were beyond the bay and then he resumed his Diamond form, and sparkled at the prow of the boat. The strong currents of the open sea rocked the boat, and waves smacked against the side, spraying them with sea water.

"Take this," Charlie said, sparking. Alan found a sliver of glass in his hand.

"Is this?" Alan stopped. He was unsure of how to phrase the question, *Is this part of you?*

"Yes," Charlie said. "Keep it safe. I'd like it back. Place it carefully on the prow. Don't worry, it will stay wherever you place it."

Alan did as Charlie instructed. The sliver of Charlie looked as if the slightest swell would knock it out of the boat and pitch it into the sea, but trusting Charlie, he left it there and returned to his seat. Charlie muttered something, and immediately the boat began to surge through the water once more.

"On course for Thule," Charlie said. "Get under the awning. It's going to get very hot."

The twins obediently sat in the shade at the back of the boat.

"But there's a lovely fresh breeze," Cathy said. "I'm not hot at all."

"The breeze masks the heat, and you don't want sunstroke," Charlie said. "Where we're going, there'll be nothing but sun."

"I thought you couldn't come with us," Alan said.

"I'm going as far I can. The most easterly point of the Diamond realm is an island, halfway between Zania and the country of Thule," Charlie said. "We'll rest there tonight, and tomorrow you must travel on without me."

"I wish you were coming with us," Cathy said tearfully.

"So do I, Cathy," Charlie said.

The sun was low in the sky when Alan spotted a long swathe of green in the middle of the sea. It sloped gently to a peak in the centre, and tapered off at either end. Diamond-shaped, like Charlie said. Alan was glad to see the island. Not that he was sick of the sea, but it was a step closer to their destination. A day and a half had already passed since the attack.

Charlie ran the boat gently to the shore, so the twins scrambled out on to the shingles and hauled it a little farther out of the water.

"Leave that little bit of me in it, and it will be safe," Charlie said.

Alan looked in awe at the little piece of Diamond that had propelled the boat across the sea. He really hoped that Charlie would send it with them on their journey. He couldn't see how they would row across the sea to Thule otherwise.

"Is it *really* a part of you?" Cathy looked wide-eyed. "What will happen when you turn back to a canoe?"

"Hopefully I'll still have all four feet," Charlie said, with a wink.

Under direction from the Diamond, the twins gathered up some driftwood and prepared a fire, for despite the heat of the day, the night would be cold. Alan then fetched the Diamond sliver from the boat, and Charlie showed him how to send a spark from it to the wood, which immediately caught.

"Sometimes it helps to recite a few words," Charlie said. "Something like this:

Splinter of light
Protect from ire
Shard so bright
Provide some fire"

"What if we're too hot?" Cathy said.

"Try this:

Splinter of light
Protect from ill
Shard so bright

Send a chill."

"I get the idea," Alan said. "If we are frozen but can't light a fire, we should say:

Splinter of light
Protect from harm
Shard so bright
Keep me warm"

"That's it," Charlie said, retreating as the blaze took hold. "Put it back in the boat now. It will be useful where you're going. Also, if you need me, grip it between both thumbs and send me a message."

After this, they toasted bread and warmed up some pie that Bens had given them. It felt like a feast, especially with Charlie telling funny stories until Alan and Cathy couldn't stop laughing. Unlike his twin, Alan didn't mind travelling to Thule without Charlie. Hadn't they survived well in the Great Forest on their own? He was confident they would succeed in Thule as well.

Charlie woke them in the cold pre-dawn light.

"What time is it?" Alan stifled a yawn as he got to his feet.

"Just gone four. The sun rises and sets early in these parts. You want to arrive after the mid-day heat and before night falls. I'll instruct the boat to travel as fast as possible," Charlie said.

"Alan, there's a fresh water stream near the hill to refill your water bottles. Come on, Cathy, time to go."

Charlie sounded anxious so Alan grabbed the canisters and ran off to the stream. By the time he came back, Cathy had rolled up their blankets, and Charlie was in his canoe form, all four feet clearly visible though sinking a little in the shifting sand.

Alan kicked grit over the last few embers. "What do we do when we reach Thule?"

"Find the Nuone city in the desert," Charlie said. "I suspect that's where the compass will send you. Ask them for their help in breaking a Thulian trapping spell. If they don't know how, or if they seem in any way dangerous, leave as quickly as possible and come back here."

"Right," Alan said. It seemed straightforward and he was confident they would succeed. He pictured returning triumphantly to Mount Slant waving a release spell and saving the Diamonds as well as his sisters.

"But the Nuones are good, aren't they?" Cathy said anxiously.

Charlie hesitated.

"They have no reason not to be. They keep to themselves mostly. Don't worry, your compass would never send you into the thick of danger."

"It might," Alan said thoughtfully. "If there was no other way."

Cathy frowned at him. "It never has before."

"The Nuones may help or they may not, but they won't harm you," Charlie said firmly. "I'll escort you around to the far side of the island. Look after that little chip of mine."

"I will." Alan was determined not to lose a second magical item.

The twins climbed into the boat, and Charlie shoved them into the sea. A light breeze sprang up as the vessel sailed parallel to the island. Charlie swam easily beside them.

They rounded the narrow tip of the island.

"I'll wait here for you," Charlie said.

"Any last words of advice?" Alan said.

"Trust your instincts, that's what I'm doing." Charlie winked. Then he gave the command to his Diamond chip, and the boat sped off across the waves, heading for Thule.

Chapter Eleven

THULE

It was mid-afternoon before a long yellow streak appeared on the horizon, the first sight of land. Cathy checked her compass before she was sure she was staring at Thule.

"At last!" she said. Despite staying beneath the awning for the entire trip, her arms were burnt, her face felt hot, and she was tired of the boat. A little knot of anxiety remained in her chest at the thought of approaching Thule without Charlie but she trusted the Nuones would help and soon she and Alan would be sailing back to Nivram with a means of breaking the Thulian spells.

As they neared land, she saw long golden beaches and high sandy cliffs, but no sign of life or habitation. A little while later, the boat ran gently aground on the sand. Alan jumped out into the shallow water to drag the boat up the shore. Cathy removed her shoes and stockings and followed. The boat was heavier than it looked, and it took all their efforts to haul it onto the soft dry sand.

"Will it be safe here?" Cathy said, worried the boat would be swept away by the sea.

"We're above the high tide mark, see." Alan pointed to a dark line that stretched across the shore. Seaweed and shells were scattered below it, but above it the sand was dry and powdery. He pulled out the anchor and tried to wedge it firmly in the ground, but the sand was too soft for a good hold.

The tiny sliver of Diamond at the prow sparkled in the sunlight.

"We can't leave Charlie's gift here," Cathy said.

"No, but I have an idea." Alan raised his voice. "Will you please settle the boat so that she won't be removed accidentally by the tide?" He tried a verse next.

"*Splinter of light*
Protect from fear
Shard of light
Keep the boat here."

At this, the boat moved forward, as if pushed by Charlie, and ploughed a few inches deeper into the sand.

Cathy nudged Alan in delight as he reached forward to pick up the chip. "Nice! Thank you, Sparkie." She had already named the little piece of Charlie.

The compass had directed them to land at this particular part of the beach, but Cathy couldn't see why. A line of sand cliffs backed the strand, stretching into the distance. Studying the compass, she saw the dial moved slowly from east to south-east, as if it didn't matter whether they climbed the sand cliffs straight ahead or wandered down the beach.

"Which way?" Alan said.

"Should we walk along by the sea for a while? The cliffs might be easier to climb later." A soft red feather, drifting in the breeze, landed at Cathy's feet. She picked it up. It felt soft between her fingers and on impulse she put in into her pocket.

"I hope the cliffs aren't magical," Alan said as they set off. "You know, ones that can't be climbed."

Cathy didn't think the compass would have sent them towards a magical barrier. They walked below the tide mark, where the sand was compact, although occasionally a wave would break and swirl about their feet, entwining their toes with seaweed. The sun beat down relentlessly, and even with their wide-brimmed hats the twins felt its force.

"Is that a gap?" Alan pointed to a dark shadow on the golden cliffs. "Maybe there's a way to the top of the cliffs?"

Cathy squinted. "Could be."

"Let's check it out. Come on." Alan grabbed Cathy's hand and pulled her along.

Alan was right. A small crevice broke the uniformity of the sand cliffs. Cathy followed him through the narrow opening into welcome shade. A shallow fissure quickly ended in a rocky sandy wall.

"I can climb this." Alan reached up, gripped a protruding rock and pulled himself up.

Although out of direct sunlight, it was stifling in the crevasse. Cathy fanned herself with her hat, watching Alan scale the wall. He disappeared from view; a few moments later a rope snaked down.

"Only use it if you really need to," she heard Alan call. "There's only me holding it here."

Cathy wasn't as good a climber as her twin, so she took her time, and only used the rope once. Eventually she clambered out of the gully and back into sunshine and gleaming white sand with glittering golden quartz.

"I knew you'd be fine," he said, coiling the rope. "I only felt the slightest tug on the rope."

"I was afraid to touch it, in case I pulled you down." She brushed sand off her hands and gazed around at the dunes. "Do we have to climb *all* of these?"

Dunes on every side reached towards the blue sky, each one taller than the last.

Alan pulled his hat out of the pocket where he had secured it before climbing up the crevasse, and tugged the brim down over his eyes. "Come on."

Cathy's muscles ached as she scrambled, slipped, and sank into the yielding sand of each dune. She soon finished one of her water bottles but it was much too hot to think of eating. At least the compass had settled on a direction of due east. As the afternoon lengthened, the intensity of the sun lessened also.

"Let's stop for a rest after this one," Alan said after about an hour.

"All right." Cathy kept her head down as she trudged onwards. She didn't think she would make it to the top as she struggled up the steep slope, but somehow she did. Gasping for breath, she reached the summit, which levelled out before dropping into a deep valley below.

"Cathy, come quickly, look at this." Alan waved his hand to hurry her up. "I think we've found the desert city."

The valley extended into the distance as far as Cathy could see, surrounded on all sides by sand dunes. In the centre of the valley, a vast lake glittered, golden in the late afternoon sun. The lake was broad at its base but tapered into the distance. In the heart of the lake was an island, triangular in shape, narrowing at the far end. Three bridges, one on each side, connected the island with the sand dunes. The island itself seemed to be a mass of shiny buildings, a golden city, surrounded by a high wall. Even the bridges appeared buttery-yellow. Cathy pulled at the chain around her neck. The compass pointed directly to the island.

With the city so near, it seemed pointless to stop, though Cathy ached with tiredness. Alan was keen to press on so she followed him. Going down the dune required almost as much effort as climbing up as the sand continually sifted beneath their feet.

Evening shadows edged across the valley, although the lake was still bathed in sunshine. As they drew close, Cathy realised the lake was more than reflecting the light of the sun. It actually was liquid gold, and she could feel heat coming off it.

Alan came to a standstill right at the edge of the lake. "Wow!"

Cathy clutched his arm. "Be careful, don't fall in. You might turn into a lump of gold this time."

"No chance. Wish I had a stick though. I'd like to stir the lake and see how thick and heavy it is."

"Come on," Cathy said, dragging him away from the edge.

The nearest bridge was on the west side of the city. Walking next to the lake, Cathy lost sight of the odd-shaped buildings. All that was visible was the soaring wall, occasionally interrupted by the smooth girth of a tower.

They stumbled onto a pathway. It felt hot beneath their feet, hotter than the dunes, and looked as if it consisted of beaten gold. They both immediately jumped back onto the cooler sand and continued beside the path.

Although Cathy could not see any activity on the lake or on the wall, nonetheless she felt unseen eyes watch as they followed the road around to the first bridge. Alan must have felt the same for he glanced frequently over his shoulder as if he expected an attack to come from the dunes.

The bridge was made of solid rock but so much gold ran through the stone that it seemed more gold than any other mineral. It was broad, spanning three arches, and at the far end Cathy saw an arched golden gate set into the city wall. A few paces from the gate, the bridge came to an abrupt end. A narrow crumbling breach fell away. It would be easy to clear, however, with enough of the bridge on the far side to land outside the gate.

At the base of the city wall, above the golden liquid, thick orange coils wrapped three or four times about the island. The girth of each loop was enormous, and trembled, expanding and contracting, as if alive.

Alan nudged her and pointed. The coils belonged to the largest snake Cathy had ever seen or could ever imagine, which had twisted its body about the base of the golden city. Its head, resting on the top loop of its body, was several times the size of Cathy. One eye was shut but the other was wide open and balefully regarding her. Then Cathy heard slithering as the serpent began to uncoil in order to launch an attack.

Chapter Twelve

PRISON DEPTHS

"**R**un," Cathy shouted. She raced back across the bridge, Alan thudding behind.

"Keep going," Alan said as he caught up. "Go to the next bridge, see if we can get into the city."

They sprinted together along the sand, the rays of the sun in their eyes as they ran towards the southern gate. After a few moments, Cathy looked back. The giant serpent was not in pursuit. She slowed, gasping to catch her breath.

"I don't want to enter the city," she said. "The compass has led us wrong. We have to contact Charlie."

Alan didn't seem worried. "That snake can only be at one gate at a time," he said. "Maybe it's a guardian of the city, like the catchills were. I hope we don't need a password to get by it."

Cathy thought she had glimpsed a hungry look in its eye. She was not going to attempt to guess any code-word. In fact, entering the city seemed like a really bad idea. Maybe the

Nuones were all snakes, wriggling in delight at the prospect of eating herself and Alan.

They rounded the corner towards the southern gate. This bridge was constructed of the same golden stone as the last, but was still intact. The coils of the giant snake pulsated gently about the island, as if the creature were breathing, but at least its head was nowhere to be seen.

"Are you ready?" Alan whispered, setting a foot on the bridge.

Cathy hesitated. Then she thought of Vicky and Susan, held by an unknown enemy, and the Diamonds trapped in their mountain. She wasn't going to let them down so she broke into a run, reaching the city before Alan. A smaller gate was set within the large city gate, both golden, both inlaid with intricate patterns traced in gold, although she couldn't determine what the images were.

Alan boldly rapped his knuckles on the gate, his face twisting into a grimace as he made contact with the warm metal.

Cathy barely heard the knock, but to her surprise the inset gate opened cautiously, and a face looked out. Its skin was scaly and tinged green, the eyes dark and the snout long. Its head reached Cathy's shoulder but no higher, and a long yellow cloak was wrapped tightly about its body, leaving its hairless and knobbly cranium exposed. It looked at them curiously, more than a little suspiciously, and spoke.

"State your business."

Cathy looked at Alan.

Alan addressed the gatekeeper. "We have come here to ask your help."

The creature stared. "Speak Thulian, please. I do not understand you."

"We don't speak Thulian," Cathy said, surprised by how awkward her words sounded.

"You are speaking it now," the gatekeeper replied.

Alan stared at her. "*What* did you say? Can you talk to them?"

Cathy was dismayed. "Can't you?"

Alan shook his head. "I don't understand you either when you talk to him."

The gatekeeper was becoming impatient. "The sun is setting. I have no more time for this. State your business or depart."

"We have come to ask your help," Cathy said. Why could Alan not communicate with the creature when she could? "Please."

The creature's black eyes flickered from one twin to the other. "Very well. I will take you to the masters." He stood back and pulled open the door.

A blast of heat buffeted Cathy in the face as she stepped through.

"Wow," she heard Alan murmur behind her as the small gateway slammed shut.

Cathy had never seen such a place. The buildings were made of metal, with tall narrow golden columns supporting raised areas wrought of elaborate designs. Equally intricate were the screens that provided the only walls or divisions. The houses were more like platforms than buildings, but the metal retained great heat from the day. Many creatures similar to the gatekeeper, Nuones she supposed, lay prostrate on the platforms soaking up the sun's dying rays.

"Follow me," the Nuone said, walking along the narrow street.

Cathy grabbed Alan's arm and followed, aware of curious eyes watching their progress.

"How do you understand them?" Alan said. "Why can't I?"

Cathy didn't know. "Unless it's my compass? Maybe it is Thulian as well?"

The street wound through the city, eventually ending in a huge arena. In the centre of this was a high dais with three thrones on top and flights of steps leading up on three sides. Dozens of unlit lanterns were positioned around its perimeter. Towering above the seats, raised high on three poles, was a huge oval shape. It might have been for shade, but it reminded Cathy of a golden nest. The sides were high, obscuring any view of anyone, or anything, that might be inside.

Three Nuones sat on the platform. Each of them wore a different coloured cloak, one was gold, one white, and one crimson, their hoods pushed back. She noticed for the first time their long tails sweeping out beneath their cloaks. Glancing at the gatekeeper, he too had a tail but it was short and stubby and hidden by the yellow cloak he wore.

What looked like about fifty Nuones were lined up at the foot of the dais. They were clad in red, but their cloaks were thrown back across their shoulders and gold-red armour gleamed on their chests and thighs. Their lower legs were green-yellow and scaly, and their feet were bare. Short swords hung on either side of their belts, ready to be drawn at an instant's notice.

The gatekeeper halted at the foot of the steps.

"Approach, Lamely," the Nuone chief clad in white said loudly.

The gatekeeper muttered something in response and clambered up the steps. At a sign from the Nuone in red, a dozen guards surrounded the twins, daggers drawn in both hands.

Cathy clutched Alan's hand. "I thought they were meant to be friendly," she whispered.

"They don't know what we want," Alan said. "They're only being cautious."

Lamely reached the top of the platform and bowed low to the three Nuones seated there. Murmurs of conversation reached Cathy's ears. Then the Nuone in red waved once more, beckoning to the twins to join them.

While Cathy hesitated, one of the guards pressed the point of his dagger into her side. "Move."

The steps were wide and shallow. Reaching the top, Cathy blinked at the panoramic view of the city, the narrow streets and flimsy buildings, the golden wall, and the great sand dunes beyond. Then she felt the attention of the three masters upon her and shifted uncomfortably as she waited for them to break the silence.

Finally, the Nuone in white spoke.

"I am Carune of the Nuones. This..." he indicated his companion in red, "...is Barne of the Nuones." Both Nuones bowed. The one in gold was not introduced.

Alan nudged Cathy, and she stumbled into speech. "My name is Cathy. This is Alan, my brother. We are from Lowdar, in Nivram."

"And why have you struck at our realm?" Carune asked.

"We haven't!" Cathy said indignantly. "We've come to ask for help. Our sisters were kidnapped, and the Diamonds have been attacked. We're hoping you can help us free them."

"This is a subterfuge, a trick," the red-attired Barne said. "They want to place their spies among us, learning our ways, ready to attack as we weaken." He glared angrily at Cathy.

"Tell him what happened," Alan muttered.

"We saw Susan and Vicky disappear. When we ran up to the Rock of Diamonds to tell Lucky, we found an invisible barrier blocked the entrance, with all the Diamonds stuck inside. Except Charlie, who said it was Thulian magic and we should ask you for help." Cathy paused to take a breath. "So here we are."

At this, the Nuone in gold leaned forward and spoke in a lighter sweeter tone.

"You believe *Nuones* attacked you by using ancient Thulian magic?" A vein of humour ran through her tones. "How ridiculous."

"We don't know who attacked us," Cathy said. "But if you won't help us, tell us where to find someone who will."

"They're spies," Barne roared. "Kill them."

"If their story is true, we should perhaps investigate it," Carune said. "Someone using Thulian powers…"

"We know we have enemies. I say get rid of these before they can harm us," Barne said.

"Silence," the golden robed one spoke. "What is that I see protruding from your pocket?"

Cathy glanced down. She had forgotten about the feather she had found on the beach. She pulled it out of her pocket. "I found it on the sand."

The feather gleamed red-gold in the setting sun. All three Nuones inhaled sharply.

"Lock them up," the gold clad one said.

"Burn them! Blast them!" Barne shrieked.

"We must interrogate them," Carune said.

"The hour of sunset approaches," the gold one said. "We have no time for cross-examination. Decide their fate this moment, not tomorrow."

"They must die," Barne said. "Too many of our foes live."

Carune hesitated. "I say wait for the morning to choose. Hasty decisions lead to trouble."

The golden clad Nuone looked contemptuously at Carune.

"Indecision is the greater enemy. Too soft as ever, Carune. Mine is the decider. Execution at first light. You may select the appropriate method, Barne. Take them away."

Cathy gasped. "We haven't done..." Guards roughly grabbed her arm and she broke off mid-sentence.

"Send them to the deepest, coldest dungeon," Barne ordered.

"But..." Cathy began, but was hustled away, hurried down the steps and through the narrow streets. Among the skeletal structures the Nuones favoured, one building stood out. Although also made of gold, it was the only one with full walls and a door. It was a relief to get out of the stuffy streets, though, even as she was shoved through the door into its shadowy interior.

A hatch in the floor was lifted up, revealing a flight of steps.

"Down," the guard said, looking anxiously over his shoulder at the fading sunlight.

The steps were steep and descended into darkness but the guard seized one of the torches by the door and held it up. Cathy had to duck her head to avoid hitting it against the low ceiling, the air growing cooler until it felt chilled. At first Cathy welcomed it, but soon she began to shiver.

The stairs finally came to an end in front of a large metal door. One of the guards pushed past Cathy, waved a hand, and muttered a few words. Locks clicked open, bolts scraped back, and the door swung open. All Cathy could see was a grey cement-like floor disappearing into blackness. Her nose wrinkled at the dank smell, which was mingled with another odour, something that resembled decay.

Then she felt Alan stumble in behind her, and the door shut with a clang.

They were left alone in the dark.

Chapter Thirteen

INSIDE THE PALACE

Paul stared out the window of his apartments. For once, the sight of the well-ordered gardens, the sun gleaming on the white battlements, and the distant copper rooftops of his city did not please him.

Since his return to his palace he had not been allowed to leave his rooms. In vain he'd told Reece that he was being escorted back to his country by a friend, that he had been rescued from the evil machinations of Queen Rose weeks earlier, and that Tremere should be released instantly. His regent laughed in reply and said he was obviously so afraid of his captor he was covering up the true story.

A day later she told him that Tremere had been released and sent back to his own country. The penalty of death would be his if he dared cross the border again.

"In the meantime," she said, "I have doubled the guards for your protection, lest another attempt be made upon your life."

Paul asked if he could at least frequent the palace grounds, but Reece told him if he needed fresh air he could visit the roof garden.

"For your own safety."

He was sick of hearing her say that.

His rooms opened onto the lower roof garden and from there he could see many guards parading along the battlements. He frowned. He hated the sight of them. Once he had taken pride in watching the palace guard in their blue and gold costumes go through their paces, but their actions had been formal and decorative, not military. These new palace guards were different. Reece had given them a black and silver uniform, and, heavily armed, they marched purposefully, as if eager for a fight.

"How long was I away?" he muttered. "Three months? How dare she change everything!" After all, he was the prince, he should decide these things.

Of course, at only a year or two older than Paul was now, Reece had stepped in as regent and stopped the fighting that the country had fallen into after his father's murder. She had taken command of the army and swiftly won victory over the rebels. By the time Paul was old enough to learn his history, peace was well established. Once hovering on civil war, that time was now only a faint memory to most of his citizens.

Although Paul suspected Reece's expanded army and heavy tactics reminded his people of those former times...

The prince turned away from the window. His sitting-room was bright and airy, with deep couches and soft armchairs, the finest quality furniture, and thick carpet beneath his feet. Vases filled with flowers from the roof garden brought colour to an otherwise white room. Doorways at the eastern end led into other rooms; bedroom, bathroom, dining room, schoolroom, and playroom. The sitting room was for more formal visits, such as those he endured from his regent. It also contained the main entrance to his apartments, or his prison, as he now termed his rooms.

It was time for his guards to change. Right on schedule he heard the approaching boots, voices in the hallway, the clink of iron, and then receding steps. He waited for a few minutes to ensure that the earlier shift had left. Then he opened the door.

Immediately spears snapped across the doorway, crossing each other at angles, and his exit was blocked.

"It is I, Prince Paul," Paul said with as much dignity as he could muster.

"Good afternoon, Prince," one of the guards said. "I'm afraid we cannot allow you leave."

"I order you to let me pass," Paul said.

"We have a sacred duty to protect your person, your highness," the guard said.

"For your own safety," the second one added.

"Very well." Paul stepped back and shut the door. He tried to leave every time they changed the guard. On each occasion different men came on duty, none of whom he recognised.

It was very frustrating, but he would work out a way to leave. He knew he would.

Tremere opened his eyes with difficulty. Some substance, now dried, had stuck his eyelids together. He could only assume it was blood. His head ached, his lip was cut too, and he was conscious of a raging thirst.

It took a few minutes for his swimming head to settle and to recall what had happened. How long he had been held? He remembered an interrogation session that ended with blows and unconsciousness. Water dashed in his face to bring him back. More interrogation.

He tried to move, wincing in pain, but something prevented him. He was shackled, at wrist and ankle. His arms and legs were numb.

He'd be lucky to escape from this without permanent physical damage.

Anger at his incarceration flooded through him but his confusion was greater. Why would he be treated like a criminal, and a dangerous one at that? Could it be for the crime he committed years earlier in Lowdar, of which he had no memory? Hardly. It was Paul's people who had arrested him. Why would they care, even if they knew, about his past?

But nothing else made any sense. He closed his eyes, leaned his head against the wall, and tried to sleep.

A little while later he heard the door of the prison cell opening. He didn't move. He'd welcome the dash of cold water. Perhaps he could gather some of it on his lips and relieve his thirst.

Voices. The first, a woman's.

"He looks in a bad way. Have we been torturing him?"

The second voice was more difficult to place, soft and jarring at the same time. "Standard interrogation methods. He is unharmed."

Tremere did not agree but preferred not to speak to his captors.

"You should clean him up. That dried blood looks revolting."

"Appearances are irrelevant. Never trust a criminal," the second voice said.

"I suppose you are right. Well, what's keeping you? Go ahead and wake him."

Cold water splashed Tremere's face. His swollen lips tried to part, to catch a few drops of the precious liquid, but failed to open before the water dripped from his chin.

"Water," he croaked.

"You have correctly identified the substance..." the second voice began, but the woman interrupted him.

"He's thirsty, can't you see?"

Tremere opened his eyes to see a young woman bend over him, holding a glass to his lips. He drank it gratefully, eager to soothe his parched throat. The woman looked familiar. Then he remembered the capture in the forest. Paul's regent, Reece.

His lips twisted into a smile.

She noticed. "Why do you smile so sarcastically? That is not gratitude."

Tremere had been thinking how strange it was that the first woman he had seen in five years was one to have him imprisoned and beaten. She was young too, and would have been beautiful only for her eyes. They were the emptiest, most vacant eyes he had ever seen in a human being. Maybe all women were like that.

He couldn't recall any specific woman from his past life, except the children's mother: Remira.

"Why...am I being held here?" His voice was hoarse, and it hurt his throat to speak. "I have done nothing to you."

She looked at him coldly. "You know quite well what you have done. Our prince disappeared three months ago. We find him, eventually, in your company. We need to know who you are working for."

"Nobody. I was escorting Paul home when you jumped us. Ask Paul. He'll tell you the same story. Now please release me."

"What insolence." She frowned and turned to her companion. "To speak of his royal highness in that manner, such familiarity. I can do nothing with him. You were right, Sylverine."

"I may proceed with the treatment?" Sylverine hissed excitedly.

For the first time, Tremere looked at the regent's companion. He was much shorter than Reece but too tall for a Nilken. A cloak of golden brocade covered him completely, the hood overshadowing the face, and hem trailing the floor. Tremere frowned. Had his captors' blows damaged his eyes? He was sure he glimpsed a long green snout beneath the cowl. No smiling Nilken but a different sort of creature altogether.

"Very well." Reece stepped back from Tremere, her expression as vacant as her eyes.

From beneath his cloak, Sylverine produced a small lantern. Muttering words Tremere couldn't catch, he swung the lantern before Tremere's face. It issued an oily green smoke, which drifted to the ground. It smelled of fire, of smelting gold, and some other scent Tremere could not identify.

"This is the fire of Thule," Sylverine droned. "And by its flame, you shall heed my words. What is your name?"

Was this a feeble attempt to hypnotise him? Tremere did not answer. Instead his mind turned to escape. The single tiny barred window set high above his head did not look promising.

"What were you doing with our revered prince? Admit that you were involved in his kidnapping."

The only furniture in the room was a narrow bunk where he sat, his hands manacled to the wall, his feet tied to the floor in a similar fashion. At least the irons that held his wrists were loose enough so that he could rest his hands on his knees. There wasn't much give in the chains that bound his legs though.

"Who was behind it? Was it the Diamonds? Admit the Diamonds instigated his kidnapping."

Tremere looked up angrily at this. "The Diamonds rescued Paul from a spell some witch put on him. Probably a friend of yours."

Sylverine turned away. "He's resisting."

"How is that possible?"

"He must be holding some talisman that protects him. Empty his pockets."

"Me?" Reece looked taken aback.

"I cannot," Sylverine snapped. "Are you afraid?"

"Of course not." An expression of distaste crossed her face as she stepped forward to Tremere.

"Go ahead," Tremere said. "You won't find anything of value."

She put a hand gingerly into one of his jacket pockets and withdrew a rusted knife. Her eyes flashed with anger. "You allowed him to keep this?"

Sylverine shrugged. "He's too well manacled to do much damage."

"You mean, it wouldn't matter if I lost a soldier or two. Well, he could have attacked me earlier."

"Wasted opportunity," Tremere muttered.

Once her search was complete, a little pile of items sat on the windowsill. The knife, a small flask, a shaving mirror, a drawstring bag, a leather purse containing a small amount of coin, some twine, and a silver locket.

Reece opened the locket and gazed at the two tiny paintings within. "He's quite handsome. She's pretty, unusual looking. Wife?"

"Sister-in-law."

"Then that's your brother. I see a slight resemblance all right." She shut the locket and dropped it on the windowsill. "His pockets are now empty, although none of these items look of interest. Try it again."

Sylverine once more raised the smoking lantern, but this time the smell confused Tremere, making him doubt himself.

"What is your name?"

"Tremere," Tremere said, surprised by his answer.

"Why did you kidnap his highness, Prince Paul?"

Tremere could not remember why he had done it. "I...don't...know," he said with difficulty. "Why...would I?"

"Because you are working for someone else. Who do you take your orders from? Is it the Diamonds?"

"No." Tremere roused himself with an effort. "No, the Diamonds rescued him." He remembered that much.

"From who?"

Tremere had to confess he didn't know. "Can't remember."

"Who instructed you to bring the prince into this country? Were you doing it for the Diamonds?"

"Yes. Lucky asked me." That much he could recall.

"So you *do* work for the Diamonds." Sylverine glanced at Reece.

"As we expected," she said.

Tremere supposed he did.

"What is their plan? Are the Diamonds going to attack this country?" Sylverine persisted.

"I don't know." Tremere tried to concentrate. He knew he was not answering the questions correctly, but he could not put his finger on what he was doing wrong. "They didn't tell me."

"A small cog only," Reece said scornfully. "Enough questioning, Sylverine. Now we know for sure the Diamonds are plotting against us. You were right, I was wrong."

Sylverine extinguished the lantern. The heavy smoke lay entwined about Tremere's ankles. He felt sleepy and closed his eyes.

"We must make a pre-emptive strike, before they attack us," he heard Sylverine say.

The regent sounded doubtful. "Is that wise? They have...certain powers."

"I have a friend who will help us negate whatever magic the Diamonds throw at us. And I am not without ability myself."

Tremere felt himself drift into sleep, despite the discomfort of his position. He was sitting at a table on a street corner, watching soldiers herd men away. A little boy handed him a keepsake. He promised to take care of it. Keep it safe from enemies. But why were the Diamonds planning to attack Prince Paul's country? It made no sense whatsoever.

Chapter Fourteen

HEALING

The healing chamber was an enormous cavern in the heart of the Rock. Tier after tier was filled with Diamonds, all moving, glowing, and changing colours in time together as they sang the low sweet song of healing.

Lucky looked at the lightless form of her father. She could never have imagined him so weak and defenceless, and she feared for him more than she had for anything in her life. Next to her father, she was the most powerful Diamond, and could do most to save him, and so she concentrated her whole being on restoring his light. Unfortunately, his injury could not have come at a worse time. It left her with neither time nor energy to solve the attack on the Rock and free the Diamonds from their imprisonment. Few Diamonds ever left the Rock, so it was not an incarceration that upset many of them. Lucky, however, fretted over her friends outside, who might be in trouble.

It reassured her to see Charlie on the plateau with the twins. He would look after them, and their sisters. Help them hide from the enemy. She trusted he hadn't thought of chasing after the attackers. He would not be strong enough to deal with them on his own. Perhaps he would think of travelling to Thule to get help. She hoped not. If the Nuones were the aggressor, Charlie would risk all but achieve nothing, and if the Nuones knew nothing about the attack, what help would they be?

Who was this new enemy who dared to attack the Diamonds? Their only known adversary was Witch Rose. Her expulsion from Nivram would not prevent her from performing mischief. Lucky pondered on the possibility that Witch Rose was behind the attack.

A soft cry from one of her sisters snatched Lucky's attention.

The king was no better, even perhaps a little worse, hovering on the brink of extinction. Lucky regretted allowing her mind to wander, and immediately renewed her concentration. The children, Charlie, their enemy, all would have to wait.

After a little while, she could see her father's faint luminance. He was approaching the turning point, but oh so slowly.

"Princess." One of the Diamonds addressed her. "Dulstar is without the chamber. He wishes to speak to you most urgently."

"Did you tell him that I could not be disturbed?"

"Yes, Princess, but he says that he cannot wait."

"Since he may not enter the healing chamber, and I cannot spare a moment from it, ask him to send a message."

The young Diamond returned a few moments later, and whispered to Lucky. "He says where does the primary duty lie?"

The Diamonds were guardians first and foremost, and should never put personal feelings ahead of their main responsibility to the good of the realm, not even to save the life of a parent. Although Lucky had been taught this precept, she did not agree with it. Besides, with their dominions under attack, her father would be needed to defeat such a powerful enemy. Moreover, her father had withdrawn from his guardianship of the peoples and creatures that lived in his realm for many years, concerning himself mainly with Diamond affairs. To him, his primary responsibility was to his own species. Lucky was only following suit, but she would not say that to Dulstar.

She sighed. "Take my place, will you, Lucent? Put all your energies into it. My father's life hangs by a glimmer. I shall not be long."

Outside the chamber Lucky met an agitated Dulstar.

"Oh, Princess, I am at a total loss. I told you that I should never be able to manage it without you. The range of materials I have is much too large, and without you to direct me, I am floundering."

"Can no one else assist?" Lucky said.

"Plenty of volunteers, but to explain the type of thing we are looking for, well, it would take twice as long."

"I am certain it's a Thulian charm, and, I think, quite a strong one to repel my father's light. Keep looking, Dulstar. I shall join you as soon as I am able to leave my father. But that may not be for many hours yet." So saying, she returned to the chamber.

As the Diamond song swelled, light flew into the air and settled on the sick king. Absorbed light helped his cure, discarded light was dead and of no further use.

Lucky didn't know why light was accepted or rejected, but she knew she could produce more waves than any other

Diamond, so she kept by her father's side for many tiring hours, until finally a faint glow beat deep within the Diamond.

The king's condition had changed. For the better. Now it was a matter of time.

When Lucky finally left the healing chamber, her father's light was gradually increasing. He was recovering, though slowly, but she had lost all track of time, and was unable to say how long she had been in the chamber.

Dulstar's room was high in the Rock. Shafts of outdoor light peppered the ceiling as he worked among his books and records. When Lucky entered his room, the old Diamond was peering through a mound of papers, looking totally lost.

"Here I am, Dulstar. Let's find the answer to this spell."

Chapter Fifteen

CHES

A lan stretched out a hand and touched Cathy's hair.

"Don't move," he said. "We don't know what's ahead."

"All right," she whispered.

Alan felt for the Diamond chip. It was pleasantly warm in his hand, and when he withdrew it, the shard glowed faintly.

"Splinter of light
Protect from fright
Shard of light
Shed some light."

The splinter glowed brighter, and Alan could see Cathy's pale anxious face.

"I wish you were a little brighter, Sparkie," he said. Instantly the light shed by the Diamond sliver intensified and spread, and Alan could see the floor beneath his feet as well as the ceiling above his head. "A little more please."

Sparkie grew much brighter, lighting up the large stone chamber. Benches lined two walls, some cloths heaped on one of them, and Alan spotted a water jug close by.

Cathy sat down on the nearest bench. "Nice place they've put us in."

"At least it's dry." Alan pressed Sparkie high into the wall, where it illuminated the room without dazzling him. "And we're out of the heat of the day."

"Now I'm cold." Cathy pulled her jacket out of her rucksack and put it on. "We still have some food left, but we won't need it. Did you hear what they said?"

"Yes, when I touch you, I understand what you and the Nuones are saying." Alan sat down beside his twin and removed his backpack. "We also have water."

"Charlie was wrong." Cathy sounded devastated. "The Nuones are bad."

Alan agreed but he didn't feel despair. For the first time he could remember, he had a magical gift in his possession. He didn't believe that they wouldn't get out of this situation. With Sparkie's help, he was sure he'd find a way.

A long-drawn out sigh echoed around the prison. Alan looked at the other bunk.

The pile of rags moved.

"Eek! A rat." Cathy jumped to her feet and away from the bench.

"Hold your water bottle. Be ready to hit it if it comes near you. I'm going to..." Alan wasn't sure what he was going to do if there was a monster hidden beneath the rags but he didn't want it to sneak up on him. "...investigate."

Holding his own water canister like an axe, he cautiously approached the bunk. The heap was still now, as if it sensed his presence. Leaning forward, he snatched the top cloth, and jumped out of the way, bottle held high, ready to strike.

Nothing moved.

Removing the top layer revealed only more rags. He snatched two pieces of cloth this time. Nothing jumped out. It looked like he would have to peel off the rags layer by layer to get to the bottom of the pile.

Growing more confident, he removed more rags, stepping back each time. He stopped when a single yellow eye appeared, staring vacantly into space. The rest of the bundle was mostly arms and legs and a body.

The creature didn't appear to notice Alan. It stared past him at nothing and gave another long shuddering sigh.

"I think it's sick," Cathy said, standing behind Alan to peer over his shoulder.

"Can you talk to it, Cathy? Find out what's wrong?"

She nodded. Grasping her compass in one hand, she stepped to the bench. Alan came with her, his arm within hers so he could follow any conversation.

Cathy cleared her throat. "Hi. My name is Cathy. This is my brother, Alan. Are you all right?"

The creature did not respond.

"It's shivering. Alan, do you think it's cold? It looks like a Nuone, and they love the heat. And it's so chilly down here."

"Let's put the covers back on." Alan picked up the rags he had earlier removed. "It must have buried itself beneath them for warmth."

They carefully wrapped the clothes around the creature, this time leaving its head clear. It had the same knobbed skull, scaly skin and long snout of the other Nuones, though its colouring seemed much paler, almost white.

For a while the twins said nothing, simply watched the creature. Every so often, it drew a long shuddering sigh, and only for that sound, Alan would have thought the creature already dead.

"Do you think it's dying?" Cathy said.

"Yes," Alan said. "We're too late to save it."

"What about Sparkie? Didn't Charlie say his present could warm us at need?"

Alan clapped her on the shoulder. "Sometimes I think you're a genius as well."

"As well as what?"

"As well as me. That's a great idea." He ran over and plucked Sparkie off the wall and closed his hand about it. His fingers glowed red. What had Charlie said? As he repeated the words, he pleaded with the Diamond chip to help.

Instantly his hand grew warm.

"It's working." He sat on the edge of the bench beside the creature and pressed Sparkie into the wall before it became too hot for him to hold. Warmth spread from the chip and soon Alan had to move away and take off his jacket. He stood beside Cathy, waiting to see if the heat would help the dying creature.

It did. After ten or fifteen minutes of warmth, the yellow eye blinked. A few minutes later, the creature stirred. The vertical iris focussed on the twins, apparently fixated by their appearance. Then the creature moved beneath the pile of clothes.

Finally it spoke.

Please Sparkie, let me understand his words, Alan thought. *Let me speak his language so I don't have to cling to Cathy the whole time.*

As if it had understood and granted his request, the light from the Diamond chip dimmed momentarily before shining as brightly as before, and Alan could understand the hoarse words that fell from the lips of the strange creature.

"Great criminals indeed," it was saying, "to be banished to the depths like this."

"Oh, we're not criminals," Cathy said. "We shouldn't be here."

"Only the greatest of offences are punished by banishment to the ice prison, where the frigid claw of death awaits to claim you." It moved, as if to sit upright, before collapsing back on its bed. "Should I not fear you?"

Alan longed to say yes to this question, but he managed to restrain himself. "Who are you?"

"Ches. You may call me Ches." The creature coughed, a harsh racking sound. "Perhaps I am already dead... yes, that explains it. Dead, and damned too otherwise I would not see animals like these..."

"You're not dead," Cathy said. "And we're not animals. We're humans."

Ches looked at her and blinked. "I was in the cold throes of death, but now I feel warm, and Thulian once again."

Alan pointed to Sparkie. "We turned up the temperature in here a little."

Ches glanced at the sliver of Diamond and then back at Alan. "Magic."

"Well, yes."

Ches coughed again. "I wonder… could I trouble you for a little drink."

"Of course," Cathy said immediately. Alan saw her hand go for her canister and nudged her.

"Water jug." He nodded to the jug under the bench.

Cathy pulled out the jug and held it up for Ches to drink. Some of the liquid dribbled down his chin. It was dark and viscous. Not water. At least, not water Alan hoped to swallow.

The drink seemed to refresh the Nuone. This time he managed to push himself into a sitting position, the rags clutched tightly about his chin, and the back of his head pressed into the wall immediately below the chip.

"Thank you. I owe you my life. Barne and the others left me here to die." He shook gently for a moment. Alan thought he was going to choke. "He is in for a surprise."

"Why are you here?" Alan said. "Aren't you one of them?"

"You've met Barne?"

"And Carune," Cathy said. "There was another there too, but we didn't get her name."

"Anea. So you met the High Council, the masters of the city. No wonder you ended up in here. Only the most hardened of criminals meet the masters."

"What did *you* do?" Alan said.

A scrawny claw emerged from beneath the blankets to briefly scratch Ches's chin. "I am a scapegoat. You know what that is? Yes, the city is in trouble, and because I foresaw it, they blamed me. Locked me up to die."

"Why?" Cathy said.

Ches pondered for a moment. "Normally I would not tell Nuone business to anyone, but you did save my life. This will make us even, my debt will be repaid."

This was not an equal exchange to Alan, but he nodded anyway.

"Two days before it happened, I saw a vast cloud in the sky. That is a rarity in Thule, and alas I was the only one who saw it. No one believed me. I warned them all, even Anea, that trouble was coming our way, but they only laughed. When the firebird was taken, Barne said I knew all about it. So they locked me in the worse prison in Thule."

"What's the firebird?" Cathy said.

"Is it possible you do not know? The firebird is our gift from Thule himself. Thanks to the firebird, our rivers run gold, our days are always warm, and at night we lie protected in the great chamber. With the firebird gone, the chamber will no longer be warm, the days will chill, and the rivers run dry. We shall all die."

"Wow, sounds serious," Alan said. "Who stole the firebird?"

"If only they had listened to me." A note of anger crept into Ches's voice. "One of our most respected citizens disappeared the day the cloud passed overhead. Then others followed. I told Anea that Sylverine was up to no good, that he had not forgotten the old days, but she didn't listen. Now the firebird is gone, and they blame me."

"Who is this person and why would he steal the firebird?" Cathy said.

Ches rolled his eyes towards the jug and looked at Cathy. She bent down and picked it up for him, although this time his two skinny claws held the jug up to his mouth to drink. He drained the urn and licked his chin afterwards with a long green tongue.

"What is your tale?" he said.

Alan would like to have persisted with questioning Ches, but Cathy answered.

"Our sisters vanished, and the Diamonds were sealed inside the cavern. We think Thulian magic was used, so we came here to ask for help to release the Diamonds, and to see if you had any idea who could have stolen our sisters."

"We gave up practice of Thulian arts a long time ago. It is forbidden now. Even Sylverine would hardly dare..." Ches broke off to cough. "I am weak and tired. I shall rest now." And he shut his eyes.

Alan pulled Cathy by the sleeve and led her some distance from Ches.

"I don't trust Ches," he whispered. "What do you think?"

"I don't know. I believe his story, and he's stuck in prison like us. Those council masters wouldn't listen to us. They want us to die. I wish Lucky was here."

She looked miserable.

"Let's eat something." Alan opened his knapsack and took out some bread and cheese. Food always made him feel better, so he expected it was the same for Cathy. "What do you think that drink tasted of?"

"Poison." Cathy gave a chuckle. "Mouldy leaves and decaying mud."

"Rats' bones and rotten fish," Alan said, between mouthfuls. Cathy looked a little more cheerful in the dim light. "Do you think the person Ches mentioned attacked the Diamonds?"

Cathy chewed thoughtfully for a moment and swallowed before answering. "Maybe. We need to know more about him."

Alan yawned. The long journey from the island, the scramble across sand under the burning sun, and escaping from a monster only to be thrown into prison by the people who were meant to help left him exhausted. He stretched out on one of the benches for a snooze. "I'm going to plan our campaign of escape."

"Me too," Cathy said, moving to the next bench. Alan guessed that she was having a nap as well. The next moment he was asleep.

When he woke, he had no idea how much time had passed. He hoped it hadn't taken all night, but he felt much refreshed by his nap, and ready for action once more.

The temperature had risen considerably while they slept, and now approached uncomfortably warm. He sat up and reached for his flask, which felt unexpectedly light. Unscrewing the top, he held it up to his mouth. Nothing came out. When he held it upside-down, a single drop rolled out and splashed on the floor.

Cathy was still asleep, so he got up and shook her shoulder.

"Cathy, did you drink my water?" He was sure it had been at least half full when he stretched out on the bench.

She looked at him bleary-eyed. "What?"

For answer, he held up his empty water bottle.

"No," Cathy whispered. She unrolled her jacket, which she had been using as a pillow covering and revealed her own bottle. The reassuring sloshing of water was heard when she shook it.

"Maybe the top was loose and it leaked," she said.

"I don't think so." Alan looked over towards Ches, still sleeping. At least, he appeared to be.

Cathy gave Alan her own flask. He gratefully took a drink, a small sip to conserve the remaining supply. He was not looking forward to the hours that lay ahead without much water.

"Come on," he said, anger stirring within him. "Ches! Wake up." He stood over Ches and called his name several times before a single yellow eye opened to regard him.

"What is it?" Ches said grumpily. "I was sleeping. Could we turn up the heat a bit? I like your gadget. Can I have it?"

"Ches, did you drink my water?"

The eye glanced at the water bottle in Alan's hand, and looked away with what Alan thought was a significantly guilty look.

"What's water? I don't know. I don't drink anything I can't pronounce. Why would I? Did you see me do it?"

"We don't mind if you did," Cathy said. Alan gave her a look. "But ask us next time."

Alan held up his water bottle. "This was half full when I went to sleep."

"Oh that," Ches said as if he had only now noticed it. "I was thirsty, I admit. Well, I'm all out of gurone, that's what we live on. I thought you might have some in that bottle-y thing of yours. What a mistake! It was all down before I realised it wasn't gurone, I wonder my choking didn't wake you. I had to spit it all up. You're better off without that...what did you call it?"

"Water. We need it to live," Alan said furiously.

"I won't do it again," Ches said.

Alan was tempted to ask Sparkie to run down the heat, but he didn't want to be mean. Besides escaping was more important.

"We need your help." Alan spoke more abruptly than he had intended, still angry about the theft of his water. "Tell me what you know about this prison."

Ches's scrawny claw scratched his bumpy forehead. "It's a prison reserved for the worst of criminals. Rarely used, I'm happy to add. Though not too pleased to be the occupant now. There are others but none so deep in the earth or so cold. What more do you want to know?"

"I want to know how to get out. How do we open the door?"

"Hmm. You don't ask much, do you? It's magically locked, you know. Only the higher orders know the codes. Useless to try and break it."

"I thought using magic was banned," Cathy interrupted. "Didn't you say that?"

"No, I said Thulian arts were banned, that is, the deep magic the Thulians used. We are Nuones, trusted by Thule himself. We wouldn't beak the rules."

"What about your friend Sylverine?" Alan said.

Ches looked crafty. "That's a different tale."

"Who are the higher orders?" Alan tried to think of some way of luring a member into the prison and capturing them. Without the captive using magic or hurting them in any way.

Nothing sprang to mind.

"We are divided into orders, depending on our closeness to the original Thulians. Anea hence belongs to the top order, as she has some Thulian blood. Barne has less but still enough to ensure he belongs to the second grouping. Carune too has some original blood, as do I, but it runs thinly now. Below, Drine and Darna and some others have a claim, but it's difficult to take seriously. None below them have any Thulian blood, we call them the lower orders."

"You're one of the higher orders!" Alan said, delighted.

Ches drew himself up on the bench with dignity. "Naturally. Otherwise I wouldn't be here. How else could they suspect me of stealing the firebird unless I had the capacity to do so?"

"So you could open the door?" Alan said.

Ches looked at Alan in amazement. "Certainly not. I am a prisoner. Yes, I know the words that will release the lock, but I am much too honourable to use them to effect my own escape."

"I'm only asking you to let Cathy and me out," Alan said. They would have to slip through the city and get out the gate without being caught, but he'd worry about that once they were free from the prison. "You can stay."

"It wouldn't be safe for you to go on your own. In fact, it's impossible. This place is heavily guarded, and even if you managed to evade the sentries, you would get lost in the maze of streets. Supposing for a moment that by sheer luck you stumbled on to one of the three gates of the city, you would not be able to open it. Even if you found out the password for one, you would still have to escape from Fang."

"Who's Fang?" Alan had a feeling he knew the answer already.

The yellow eyes blinked at him. "Fang is the great snake encircling the city and eating all those who attempt to leave."

Chapter Sixteen

FANG

F ang. Alan had forgotten about the giant serpent. Fixing his eyes on Sparkie, Alan silently begged the sliver of Diamond to help them escape, to give him some idea for leaving Thule. The Nuones wanted to kill them at dawn, and it was much too unlikely to expect a change of heart. Somehow they had to break out of the prison, make their way back to the boat, and sail to Nivram.

It was at this moment Alan had his great idea.

He pointed to Ches. "You're coming with us."

Ches fell back in the bed. "What?" he shrieked. "It's impossible. Even if I opened the door, how would you get beyond the guards?"

"You said everyone goes into some warm chamber at night, didn't you?"

"I may have. Yes, that's true. Even though it is losing its heat without the firebird, the outside temperature is still much colder."

"Do the guards go in as well?" Cathy said.

Ches nodded. "The night air would surely kill them otherwise."

"Then we'd get through the city without being seen. Perfect." Despite the serious situation, Alan couldn't help grinning.

Ches looked at Alan with misgiving. "I would die. I cannot survive in that cold night air."

"You will with our help." Alan said. "Sparkie will keep you hot."

"Brilliant." Cathy thumped Alan's arm. "Then what?"

"Ches will guide us through the city to the best gate to exit, so we won't meet the giant snake."

"Fang." Cathy nodded, as if she knew the beast personally. "You can open the gates as well, can't you, Ches?"

"Wait a moment, wait a moment." Ches was getting agitated. "If I help you escape, I'll be in even worse trouble than I am now. My death will be even more lingering and torturous."

"Couldn't you let yourself back into the prison?" Cathy said.

"Only if I keep your portable heater. I would not last a minute without it."

"Oh," she said.

"Doesn't matter," Alan said, keen to unveil his inspiration. "You're coming back to Nivram with us, Ches."

The Nuone made a snorting sound, and Alan realised that the creature was laughing.

"Why would I do that? Leave my homeland? Go to the wild northern lands, where the nights are long and cold? I don't think so."

"But they're going to kill you here," Cathy said.

"Our friends are sealed inside their homes," Alan said, refusing to believe that Ches would rather die than go with them. "It's like an invisible force, you can't see it, but you can't get past it either. We think it's your kind of magic."

"Are you expecting me to break it open?" Ches rubbed his snout with a wizened claw.

"Yes," Alan said firmly. "Can you?"

Ches pushed away the blankets and basked in Sparkie's warmth. His tunic was red, buckled with a silver belt, but his feet were bare. Alan counted three large toes, or claws, on either foot.

"Tell me more about yourselves. I'm not familiar with these Diamonds you mention."

"I don't know how to describe them," Cathy said. "They're the guardians of Nivram."

"And how do you know such powerful beings?" Ches looked craftily as her, as if he didn't believe her.

Cathy rushed into a shortened version of how they met Lucky and travelled to the Rock of Diamonds, and then how Queen Rose had attempted to seize control of the country but was defeated.

"She's been banished from Nivram now," Cathy finished with, "so we knew it couldn't be her who attacked us."

"I love a story with a happy ending," Ches said. Alan wasn't sure if he was being sincere. His suspicions of Ches remained, but it seemed too good an opportunity not to take the Nuone with them.

"Tell us more about the Nuones," Cathy said. "And the firebird, whatever that is."

"Quickly, then, for the night is passing and we need to be gone by daybreak," Ches said. "When the original Thulians fell out of favour with Thule and were punished, he allowed their servants, the Nuones, distant kinsfolk, to remain. Some inter-marriage had occurred in the old days, hence some Thulian blood remains. This is how we have some base magic. It is forbidden to call up the higher levels, even if we knew how." He broke off to cough.

Alan waited impatiently for Ches to continue. Somehow, he felt, they were getting close to the truth.

"What's this got to do with the firebird?" Cathy said.

"After the great purge, Thule left us with both our firebird and our snake to ensure our good behaviour. Fear of the firebird prevents Fang leaving his nest in the desert. Now the firebird is gone, Fang slowly crushes the city, eating those who try to escape."

"Who took the firebird?" Cathy said.

"Ahh. If we only knew that," Ches said sadly.

"So either your own people will torture you to death, or you'll die of the cold when the night chamber loses its heat, or else Fang will eat or crush you?" Alan said. "Doesn't seem much of a choice. You should leave with us."

"You have a delightful way of putting things," Ches said sourly. "Very well, I shall come with you. I am slightly intrigued by your problem. Sounds like a level two or three spell. I may be able to help."

"What about Fang?" Cathy said. "How can we get past him?"

"He has a single head," Ches said. "He can guard only one gate at a time, though he moves rather quickly. I imagine when the time comes for a great exodus out of the city, my people will divide into three groups, one for each gate, and leave at the same time. That way, some will surely make it into the desert..." He paused to clear his throat. "Where Fang will follow to devour the last of them after the city lies in dust."

"So we may as well take our chance with Fang," Cathy said.

"Probably dead either way," Ches agreed. He swung his feet to the floor and tentatively stood up. "Good. They still work."

They worked all right when you stole my water, Alan thought, but let it pass. Ches seemed to have an idea of the passing of the night. "How are we doing for time?"

Ches sniffed the air. "The heat is distracting me." He walked towards the door and inhaled deeply. "Almost light. We should go. Now."

His tone was urgent, so Alan and Cathy picked up their jackets and rucksacks, and Alan plucked Sparkie from the wall.

"Here, wait," Ches said. "What about heat for me?"

Alan had forgotten his promise. He didn't want to give Sparkie to Ches but he didn't have a choice. Pressing it firmly into the front of Ches's tunic, he was surprised by how tall their fellow prisoner was. The other Nuones were squat, with thick bodies that only reached his shoulder. Ches was stringier, thin and with long legs that made him taller than Alan.

"Keep Ches warm, please," he asked Sparkie, and stood back. "You should be fine now."

A smile spread across Ches's face as the warmth surged from Sparkie. "I am ready to depart. But we must hasten." He swept his claws in front of the doorway, muttering under his breath.

With a small clunk, the door swung open. "Hurry," Ches hissed, stepping out quickly.

It was dark in the passageway and winding stairs. Sparkie cast some light though Ches's bulk impeded most of it. All the same Alan managed to follow the Nuone, with Cathy hanging on tightly to his jacket.

A bitter wind swept through the city as they emerged from the prison entrance. The temperature was much colder than Alan expected, and he shivered inside his jacket. The triangular latticed houses of the city's inhabitants lay in darkness and the sky was a pre-dawn grey.

"Hurry," Ches said once more, urgency threaded through his voice. He immediately started to lope through the streets, his long legs covering the ground easily.

Alan had to break into a run to keep Ches in sight.

"Is he trying to lose us?" Cathy panted at his side.

The same thought had crossed Alan's mind. "I hope not." He thought of Ches running off carrying the fragment of Charlie. He didn't want to consider how he could tell Charlie, let alone how they would even reach the canoe on that far distant island without Sparkie.

They dodged their way through the shadowy streets as the sky brightened. The fear that at any moment thousands of Nuones would pour from their secret chamber kept Alan moving. Soon he saw the smooth white wall of the city, not yet golden in the rising sun. Ches disappeared abruptly between two houses, and when they followed him, they saw him standing in front of an enormous metal gate, with a smaller door inset.

Alan was so disoriented that he had no idea which direction they were travelling in. "Which gate is it?"

"The west. I heard the guards say that it was damaged, and no longer under surveillance."

"We met Fang there yesterday," Alan said. "And there was a gap in the bridge."

"Fang is a creature of the sun too. At night he sinks below the golden waters of the lake," Ches said. "How great is the break in the bridge? Can we jump over it?"

"*You* could step over it," Alan said.

"Fang is more likely to watch the other gates. But we must move quickly, the opening of the gate will disturb his slumbers." Ches raised his hands and waved them in front of the gate in a complicated series of gestures, all the time muttering under his breath.

Alan listened closely this time but could not understand a word.

Slowly, gratingly, the gate opened. The full gate, not the smaller one. For whatever reason, Ches had chosen to release the large gate. In the grey light of early morning, the stone bridge rushed to meet them, abruptly halting five or six foot short.

A much greater gap than the previous day.

Alan knew he could clear the distance. He looked at Cathy who nodded to reassure him.

The gates finally came to a halt, fully open, and the grinding noise ended in silence.

"Go," Ches shouted and leaped onto the bridge.

Alan hesitated, checking for Fang. The thick coils of the snake were still wrapped around the circumference of the city, but there was no sign of its head. As Alan jumped, he caught movement in the waters, ripples from a disturbance below, but he cleared the gap well. Positioning himself at the edge of the bridge, ready to extend a hand to Cathy if she got into trouble, and not daring to think what it would be like to fall into the water, he nodded at her to jump.

"Easy," he said.

Cathy stepped back a few paces before running forward and leaping into the air. As she jumped, Fang's head rose from the water below and snatched her in its jaws.

Chapter Seventeen

PAUL VISITS THE PRISON

P aul sat out in his rooftop garden among the profusion of flowers, the wealth of colours proclaiming summer had arrived. A small fountain played nearby, the tinkling of water into a stone basin designed to soothe all listeners.

Paul was far too excited to pay any attention to the fountain. It was simple to escape his apartments, and he would have berated himself for being so slow to think of it if he wasn't equally impressed by his genius. Reece's apartments shared the same rooftop gardens as his. Reece's apartments would not be guarded. All he had to do was slip into his regent's quarters when she was out.

Then he would visit the palace dungeons to see for himself if Tremere had been released or was, as Paul suspected, still held prisoner.

The early morning sun shone directly into the garden. Surrounded on one side by his own rooms, the second had windows looking into a passageway, and the third were the regent's private quarters. The fourth side of the garden opened onto a view of the city, and beyond the city walls, emerald fields, glimmering rivers, and in the far distance: blue-grey mountains. Paul had been up early and admiring the sunrise when he had seen a large contingent of mounted soldiers leave the palace and ride in the direction of the city gate.

He wasn't sure, of course, for the rising sun had blinded him, but it looked like Reece' special guard, which she always led.

Caution made him wait for the cleaning staff to first sweep and clean Reece's apartments, which was done early each morning. As an additional precaution, he had told his tutor that he was going to spend the day studying outside in the sun and did not want to be disturbed. His tutor had tried to argue the point, but when Paul reminded him of the importance of sunlight and fresh air, the tutor could only say he was grateful that Paul was paying attention to some of his lectures, and went off to enjoy his unexpected day off.

The excuse of studying outside had thus got rid of both his tutor, and any remarks the cleaning staff might make if they thought him strangely absent from his own rooms.

The garden was designed with many recessed areas, small stone benches surrounded by shrubs that provided perfect cover for anyone wishing to eavesdrop. Paul stationed himself in one such niche below the windows of Reece's study, waiting impatiently for the maids to arrive.

The sound of the door opening pleased Paul, but it turned quickly to annoyance when he recognised the voice that spoke as that of his regent.

"What is the matter, Sylverine? What is so urgent that it cannot wait until later? My regiment has ridden without me." She spoke wearily.

This was extremely irritating news. Paul had not considered the possibility that Reece might remain in her apartments all morning.

"I can only spare you a few moments," Reece continued, to Paul's relief. "I intend to catch up with my soldiers."

Good, thought Paul. *I won't have to wait long.*

A brief silence followed her words. Then Paul heard the hateful sibilant tones of Sylverine.

"I shall not delay you. I want to speak to you about the prince."

Reece made an exclamation of annoyance as Paul tensed in his seat.

"Not this again. I told you before, I do not want you to work your magic tricks on Paul."

"You didn't want me to do it on the prisoner either but look what good results we obtained."

"Why are you so keen to do it on Paul?" The regent spoke after a moment's silence. "He's only a child."

Paul bridled at this. Child indeed! Reece had not been much older when she stepped in to take charge of the kingdom.

"By your own words, I know the prince is a friend to the Diamonds, our enemies. I wish to make sure... his loyalties are correct."

How Paul would have loved to pick up a sword and drive it through that evil creature. Paul was a natural swordsman, even his fencing instructor said so. Or rather, Paul corrected himself, *could* be, if he practised. Fencing and strategy were Paul's favourite subjects.

"Loyalties," repeated Reece. After this, there followed a long silence before she spoke once more. "As you wish, but later. His tutor is with him now. In any case, I would like to be present. This evening perhaps..."

"Still resists this request, somehow," Sylverine said, as if to himself, before adding in a louder voice: "Very well. I shall attend to the prince this evening."

Paul could barely contain himself, listening to Sylverine plan to harm him, but he forced himself to sit still. Reece's door opened and closed. Paul watched out in case Sylverine ignored Reece and slipped back to find Paul directly but nobody passed through the corridor to his quarters, unless they crawled on their hands and knees below the window ledges.

He wouldn't put anything past Slithery Sylverine, so he remained on the bench and waited.

A short time later, he heard the cleaning staff enter the antechamber with a clattering of pails. One entered the study, and he heard a startled apology and the scrape of a chair.

"Come in," Reece said. "I am leaving now."

It hadn't occurred to Paul that Reece would linger after Slithery left. He heard Reece greet the maids pleasantly as she departed. At least now he was sure she was gone.

"Shall I close the windows?" Paul heard one ask. She sounded very young, a child.

"No, no." Paul recognised the voice of one of the senior housekeepers. "The regent likes plenty of fresh air, Jen."

"What about this stuff? Should I throw it out?"

"Throw nothing out," the housekeeper said. "Touch nothing except dust and dirt."

"It looks so old and dirty."

"Put it back where you found it, Jen."

"Yes, Ma." The invisible Jen sounded hesitant. Paul was curious. What was Jen talking about? Jen said no more. Neither did the housekeeper who shortly afterwards began singing an old folksong. It seemed like half the day went by before the maids left Reece's quarters, although Paul knew barely an hour had passed. A moment later he saw the stream of cleaners pass along the corridor towards his apartments.

The window beside him was ajar, and it was an easy matter to loosen the catch and open it wide. Paul climbed inside, careful to close the window over as he found it.

It was some time since he had last been in Reece's quarters, for generally the regent visited him. Her rooms were identical in design and style to his own apartments, except that hers were terribly cluttered and Paul's were kept tidy. As he slipped through her study, a small bundle sitting on top of her desk caught his eye. They must have been the dirty old items that Jen was complaining about, but Paul thought the leather purse and dagger looked familiar. Like something Tremere would carry.

On impulse, he snatched the lot up and stuffed them into his pocket. Reece's behaviour since his return meant he no longer trusted her; he could not even be sure she wouldn't rob Tremere of his few humble belongings.

The corridor outside the regent's apartments was quiet. A marble staircase descended immediately opposite her door, and

Paul ran gleefully down the steps. It felt good to be out of his room, to have outwitted Reece and Slithery.

The palace rose seven stories above the dungeons and Paul met no-one as he descended all seven flights. Reaching the foot of the stairs, Paul took the passageway to the stables. It was the longer route to the palace prisons but likely to be quieter.

His luck held out. The passageways were deserted. Paul ran across a courtyard past the stables, and through several other corridors before reaching the entrance to the prisons. A huge iron door, heavily bolted, barricaded the way. Although only one guard sat at the gate, the guardhouse was close by, and Paul knew it would be packed with soldiers.

"Morning, your highness." The elderly guard lumbered to his feet.

"Good morning." Paul recognised the heavy build and dark complexion but struggled to remember the man's name. "I'm here to see one of the prisoners, Tremere by name. He was brought in two days ago."

The guard rubbed his nose thoughtfully. "Well, your honour, I mean, your highness, that's a little difficult to tell. So many prisoners have been brought in these last few days. Quite a crowd, yes, indeed."

"The man I seek is most likely in solitude. He's highly dangerous. In fact, he was involved in my... er... kidnapping recently." Paul leaned forward confidentially. "You may have heard about that."

The guard looked a little confused. "Oh yes, indeed. I mean, I think I know as who you may be referring to. All by himself. End of the row. You'd feel sorry for him, if he weren't so dangerous."

"I need to speak with him, state business." Paul tried to sound imperious. "Perhaps you would escort me?"

"Me, your honour? I'm only a poor gatekeeper." The man looked embarrassed and delighted at the same time.

"Perfect. You may find someone to cover for you here, if you like."

The man nodded. "Best I do that."

Shortly afterwards, Paul, feeling awfully pleased with himself for being so clever, walked into the dungeons. As he was escorted by the gatekeeper, none of the guards he met raised an eyebrow.

Passing cells crammed with townsfolk and country dwellers was an unpleasant experience. Sobbing women with screaming children, and men who cursed him as he passed... He felt very uncomfortable under their glares, and wondered why so many people were imprisoned. What crime were they accused of? He whispered his question to the gatekeeper, but Lenno (the name came back to him) did not know anything about them.

"I lets them inside," he said. "Occasionally I lets one outside again, but that's rare enough these days."

What upset Paul the most was the amount of abuse hurled at him. They did not seem to regard him as their beloved prince, but rather a menace and a tyrant.

All Paul's life he had been taught his duty to his people, and about the love and reverence his people had for him in return.

It looked like he had lost some of that love.

It was a relief to reach the relative silence of the singly occupied prisons. Unlike the bars of the communal cells, these had solid doors, so the prisoners could not see Paul. Here the more dangerous criminals and suspects were kept.

Lenno came to a halt at the last cell and raised a flap set into the door so Paul could peer inside. He saw Tremere seated on a bunk, arms and legs shackled to metal fastenings in the granite wall.

Anger surged through Paul at the discovery that Reece had indeed lied to him, and that his friend Tremere was still being treated like a criminal. "Open the door," he said, his voice shaking.

Chapter Eighteen

THE DAGGER

"I can't let you in, though, your highness," Lenno said. "This cell is for the most hardened and evil of criminals. He's as likely to cut yer throat as look at you. Not safe for our prince."

Paul glared at the porter. "I order you to open that door."

"I can't, your highness." Lenno looked at his feet. "I don't have the key. Only the gatekeeper, that's all I am."

"Will you please fetch it? Now. And some fresh water and bread."

Lenno gaped at him.

"Never mind," Paul said. "Please get the key. Then you may await me here. You'll see, I shall be perfectly safe with you outside the door."

"I suppose you would be." Lenno sounded pleased and plodded off to get the key while Paul waited impatiently outside Tremere's cell.

Eventually footsteps echoing along the passageway announced Lenno's return. Paul curbed his tongue while the gatekeeper slowly fitted a large iron key to the first lock, and two more to the other locks, and then drew back three bolts and unhooked one chain.

"This way, your highness." Lenno dragged open the door and stood back. "I'll wait here. Call if you need me."

"Thank you." Paul stepped through the doorway into the prison. He was not impressed with what he saw. Cold filthy stone. A small bunk bed against the wall. A tiny barred window high above the bed. Floor, ceiling and walls were covered with scrawled letters and markings, all a rusty brown colour, as if former occupants had written their messages in blood. The thought made him feel ill.

Tremere's arms were pulled back over his head where his fetters shackled him to the wall. His ankles were fettered beneath the bunk, forcing him into an uncomfortable sitting posture. Tremere's eyes were closed, as if somehow he had managed to get to sleep.

Paul waited until the door had shut behind him and then he ran forward.

"Tremere, it's me, Paul." He sat beside the prisoner on the hard mattress and spoke low. When Tremere didn't stir, the prince tugged on his shoulder. "Tremere," he said, a little louder.

Tremere's eyes blinked open. With a few days' growth on his chin, bloodshot eyes, and a crust of dirt and grime across forehead and cheeks, partly covering an angry bruise, Tremere looked a mess.

"Your...highness." Hoarse words fell from cracked lips. Tremere made a move as if he wished to stand, but his restraints prevented him.

Paul reached for a jug of water and held it to Tremere's lips. He would have words with whoever looked after the dungeons. Reece would be furious too.

Tremere drank gratefully.

"Thank..." He cleared his throat. "Thank you."

"I've come to get you out of here." It didn't look like it would be easy.

"The Diamonds sent me," Tremere said.

"I know, I was there. Remember?"

Tremere shook his head. "Why are they going to attack you?"

"Who?" Paul pulled at one of the iron rings with all the strength he could summon. It didn't budge.

"The Diamonds. They have a plan."

"That is ridiculous. Lucky is our friend. Why would she attack?" Paul dropped to his knees and looked under the bed. He made a face. The floor was filthy, covered with refuse and cobwebs, and it stank. Disdainfully he flicked away a dead beetle with his handkerchief, before stretching out to pull on one of the heavy chains. He thought he felt a slight give. Maybe this was a weak point.

"I work for them. I know," Tremere muttered, closing his eyes.

Paul was getting irritated. "You only met them two weeks ago. What are you talking about?" He straightened up and brushed dirt off his clothes. Had prison affected Tremere's mind?

"A plot against you..."

"I am aware of it. Well, that it exists. Not what it's about. You must have met Slithery. Do you know what is going on? I think Slithery is trying to take over my kingdom. He has turned my regent against me." Paul recalled the words that Sylverine had spoken earlier. *I wish to make sure... his loyalties are correct.* Slithery had some plan involving him. One that was intended to be put in place later that evening.

It only occurred to him then that he had to get both Tremere and himself out of the palace as soon as possible. Before Sylverine corrected his loyalties.

"I have something of yours." Paul produced the items he had recovered from Reece's room. Tremere didn't respond so Paul slipped the knapsack around Tremere's neck. "I thought you would be glad to have this back." He wished Tremere was himself. Otherwise rescuing him was going to be impossible.

Tremere opened his eyes. "Paul." He sounded surprised.

"Yes." Paul sighed. "It's me."

"Have you been thrown into prison as well? What are you doing here?"

Paul was offended. "I have come to rescue you."

"Good. A royal reprieve. I told them to talk to you, that I hadn't done anything, but they seemed to think I had."

"Er, it's not quite an official release. I've come to rescue you."

Tremere looked him in the eye. "Are you not the prince of this country? Can you not command my freedom?"

"No." Paul looked at his shoes. "I am a prisoner here too, almost as much as you. I will be escaping with you."

"What happened?" Tremere's voice was kinder now, more sympathetic.

Paul sat down on the bed and told how he had been confined to his apartments, for his own protection. "Reece told me that they had let you go, expelled you from the country, but I didn't believe her. She's not the same person she used to be."

"Maybe you never saw this side of her before," Tremere said gently. "You tell me at sixteen years of age she stepped into your father's shoes and brought peace to your country? That is a remarkable feat for any person, let alone at that young age."

"She is strong and determined. Brave and courageous," Paul said, remembering how much he had admired her growing up.

"Ambitious too, I'd say. She cannot be looking forward to the day that you take charge of your kingdom."

"Slithery is a bad influence on her. He has turned her against me. Today I heard him persuade her to allow him test my loyalty." He hesitated. Sylverine scared him, but he did not want to admit that to Tremere. "I do not want to be around to find out what that means."

"Who is he? *What* is he? He came with your regent to get a confession from me."

"What did you tell them?"

"Oh, that I was a spy working for the Diamonds." Paul laughed but Tremere remained serious. "Or something like that. I told them what they wanted to hear. But enough chatter. Can you do anything to free me? I am weary of being strung up like this."

"I took no weapon with me." That was a careless oversight. Always be prepared, Paul reminded himself, even though until he had eavesdropped on Reece and Sylverine, he was only looking to see if Tremere was still in the palace.

"I had a dagger but your regent took my belongings." Tremere noticed his leather bag for the first time. "Where did this come from?"

"I found it in Reece's study." Paul opened it and pulled out the dagger. The handle was covered in grime and the blade shone dully. "Should I try unscrewing the bolts with this?"

"No, try to sever a link in the chain that binds me to the wall."

"With *this*?" Paul was sceptical.

Tremere gave a short laugh. "It's a good knife. Cuts whatever I wish it to."

"If it cuts through these chains of yours, it's a magic knife."

"Right hand first please."

"Very well." Paul knelt on the bunk, and held the blade to one of the links. Delicately at first but then with more force, he tried to carve through the link.

"Any luck?" Tremere said.

Paul shook his head. "No good. I've scraped off a little rust, but nothing more." He held up the blade so Tremere could see the brown flakes staining it.

"Can you place my dagger between my fingers?"

Paul passed over the knife. It dangled precariously between Tremere's two fingers, the tip of the blade touching the first link of the chain that bound him to the wall.

"Stand back, I might drop it."

Paul got off the bed and watched as Tremere gently swung the blade across the nearest link in the chain. He moved it slowly back and forth several times before dropping the knife. It fell with a plop on to the floor.

Paul picked it up, amazing to see that Tremere's gentle movements had carved deep scars in the metal. What kind of material was the blade made from? It looked damaged, incapable of cutting butter.

"It's working," he shouted. "Keep going."

Tremere's fingers gripped the handle once more and continued with the delicate work. Within a few minutes, he dropped the knife for the second time, but it had done its job. One side of the link had been cut through, and Paul was able to remove the chain from the handcuff. With his right hand free, it took only a few moments for Tremere to cut through the chain restraining his left, and rub his released wrist.

"That's better."

"We should hurry." What if Lenno had spied on them through the door and called for re-enforcements?

Tremere stretched down awkwardly to break the restraints that bound his feet and within a couple of minutes was standing away from the bed.

"Thank you, Paul."

"You're welcome." Paul did not point out that it was the least he might do, his own people having wrongly imprisoned him, but the thought crossed his mind.

"What next?" Tremere asked. "What kind of soldiers do you have here?"

"Numerous," Paul said.

"I was afraid you'd have that kind," Tremere said. "How can we get out?" His eyes wandered towards the window, but even Paul could see that the opening was much too small for a man of Tremere's size to squeeze through.

"I have a plan," Paul said.

Chapter Nineteen

FANG'S MAW

F ang's head reared high, the muscles of its neckless body rippling as it grasped Cathy in its mouth. She screamed as mucous dripped from its jaws, and its monstrous red eye looked venomously at Alan.

"Hang on, Cathy." Alan looked around desperately for a weapon. All he had was his rucksack. He slipped it off his shoulder, and swung with all his strength at the monster.

He missed, and swung again. Another miss.

"Come on," Ches urged. "It's too late, he's got her now. Quick, before he comes after us."

Alan ignored him and swung his rucksack once more. It hit the thick hide of the beast without any noticeable effect, other than on Alan, who, jarred by the impact, nearly dropped the bag into lake.

Cathy had stopped screaming, and was now lying limp in Fang's mouth. The giant snake weaved its head about in the air as its coils loosened around the island. It seemed it was preparing for another attack.

Alan hit out again, frustration and anger giving him extra strength, but although his arms hurt, Fang did not falter.

Cathy's water canister slipped off her shoulder and smacked the parapet of the bridge, providentially landing a few feet behind Alan as he swung fruitlessly. Her rucksack was about to follow.

"Careful." Ches spoke in his ear. "If that bag hits you from up there, your head will be smashed."

Something sparkled and caught the corner of Alan's eye. Charlie's chip, Sparkie, fastened to Ches's tunic. Alan grasped a handful of the tunic, seizing control of the chip, and directed the Diamond at the snake's red eye. "Dazzle him! Burn him! Blind him!"

"Kill him!" Ches shouted.

A bright ray of light shot through the air and engulfed the red eye. Alan lost sight of the snake's eye for a moment before its eyelid shot open once more. A dark substance leaked from its eye. Fang opened its mouth a little, enough to give a hideous hiss.

Ches jumped up and down in excitement. "That hurt him, that really did. Do it again."

"Oh no." Alan froze. Cathy had slipped out of Fang's mouth when it had cried out, only her jacket held her, caught somehow on one of the great beast's fangs. If it tore, she would drop like a stone either to smash to pieces on the bridge or to drown in the waters of the lake, now rapidly turning golden in the rays of the rising sun.

Every moment Alan expected Cathy to fall to her death.

"Cathy," he shouted, hoping to get her attention. "Wake up."

She seemed either unconscious or already dead.

"He's lowering," Ches said. "Going back to the water."

The Nuone was right. With every weaving movement the serpent made, its head dropped lower.

"I think he's coming for us," Alan said.

The red eye glared vindictively as the great snake slowly lowered its head. Alan couldn't move, his eyes fixed on Cathy. A few feet above his head, Cathy's jacket ripped and she fell towards the water. Something moved beside Alan. Quick as a flash, Ches stretched out his skinny arms and snatched her before she touched the lake.

"Now will you move?" he snarled, before turning and loping across the bridge, Cathy in his arms. Alan tore after him, seconds before the heavy head of the snake crashed down on the bridge where he had been standing.

They ran across the bridge and along the metal path that encircled the lake.

"The sea," Alan gasped. "Head for the sea."

The slithering sound of Fang unwrapping itself from the city reached his ears. There was no time to stop and see how Cathy was. Ches jogged towards the dunes. The sun had risen above the horizon, and yellow light filled the morning. Ches took the sand dunes in his stride, while Alan floundered behind him. The Nuone had large wide feet, with splayed toes able to find a good grip in the sifting soil.

When Alan caught up with him, Ches had stopped on the far side of the first sand dune and laid Cathy down. She was still unconscious, but Alan could see that she was breathing, and her cheeks were flushed. He dropped to his knees beside her.

"Can't stop long," Ches said. "The beast will see our tracks, and he moves fast."

Cathy's clothes were covered with an oily black mucous and torn at her waist where the beast first caught her.

"Will she be all right?" Alan said.

Ches shrugged. "I know nothing about your kind. You tell me."

Alan pulled her ragged shirt back a little, exposing a large gash, blood oozing from it. It looked infected. Cathy's forehead was shining with sweat, the onset of fever.

"Let us continue," Ches said. He stood up and picked Cathy up. He seemed much stronger than he looked. "Listen, we are even now. Her life for my life." He turned and stomped away.

Alan followed, numb with anxiety. Cathy was his twin, she couldn't die! He wouldn't allow it. Yet a terrible dread burned inside that she would.

He forced his mind away to another matter. Ches. Alan couldn't help suspecting Ches had chosen the exit by the broken bridge hoping one of them would fall, distracting Fang from Ches's flight. Ches had seemed so anxious to leave Cathy to the monster so he could escape. Yet Ches hadn't gone, and in the end had saved Cathy. Alan still couldn't bring himself to trust Ches. Cathy's water canister hung over Ches's shoulder, the Nuone had been quick-thinking enough to snatch it up when it fell. No, Ches had a plan.

Behind him, distant chimes clamoured.

"Good news, they've discovered our escape."

"How is that good news?" Alan panted.

"Distraction for Fang. He'll forget about us."

Alan thought of the venom in the snake's eye and shuddered. He hoped Ches was right.

The sun climbed higher in the sky. Ches seemed bolstered by all the heat but Alan found it difficult scrambling over the dunes, his eyes dazzled by the sun and the sand's glare, afraid to take a drink for he wanted to save the remaining water for Cathy, anxious to keep moving in case someone was chasing them, and terrified that the boat might have been swept to out to sea. Among all of this, he was conscious of a ravenous thirst. His head hurt.

After several hours, the dunes grew smaller, although the heat trapped between the sand hills intensified. Alan was sweltering, and he longed for the sight of the cliffs and the sea. Before he saw either, Ches darted into a narrow gully Alan hadn't noticed whose slope led gently to the shore.

In the shade of the gully, Ches laid Cathy down on the ground once more.

"You better take a look," he said roughly. His tunic was stained where he had been carrying Cathy.

Alan felt sick as he looked at his sister's pale face. Her shirt was covered in blood and her forehead was burning up.

"Water," he said.

Ches handed him the flask, and Alan tried to coax Cathy to drink, but the water dripped over her chin and fell onto the sand. He peeked at her stomach wound. It was badly infected, and the area discoloured, black with a greenish tinge. A nasty smell rose from it, and Alan quickly covered it up.

"You need to wash it out, get rid of the beast's poison," Ches said.

"We're almost out of water," Alan said bleakly, his own throat achingly dry and his lips cracked.

"Then you have no choice."

Alan did not look at him. "What?"

"You are obviously ranked higher than your sister. Plus she is already injured and will probably die. Take the water for yourself to ensure that at least one of you survives."

"That's what you would do, is it?" Alan's voice shook. He could not believe what he was hearing, and if Ches wasn't needed to break the Thulian magic, he'd have left him in the desert to face Fang.

Ches nodded emphatically. "Survival of the fittest."

Alan got to his feet. "The boat isn't far from here. Will you carry her there?"

Ches sighed. "Mistake," he said but he bent down and hoisted Cathy up without any further complaint.

It was a relief to see the deep blue of the sea and the breakers rushing into shore. If Cathy hadn't been injured, Alan would have felt pleased with himself, heading back to Nivram with a prize like Ches to unlock the Rock of Diamonds and free Yvonne. But now he couldn't feel anything except terror as he peered into the distance to spot the boat.

Ches's voice interrupted his thoughts. "Why don't you use your magic on her?"

"What magic? You mean..." Why hadn't he thought of that before? "Give me back my chip."

Ches strode across the strand. "You said I could have it to keep warm on this stupid journey of yours. I took it as payment for my services."

"No, it's not," Alan said, jogging to keep up. "It's hot now and you don't need it. I'll lend it to you when it gets cold."

"Oh, very well," Ches grumbled. But he stood still and allowed Alan remove it from his tunic.

The Diamonds had healing powers. He hoped Charlie had included some of his with the rest of his gift.

"Please, Charlie," Alan said, "Please cure Cathy. Please." He didn't know what else to say. Did the Diamond glow a little brighter or was it the sun? Either way, Cathy looked no better. After a moment they walked on.

It was Ches who spotted the boat. "Is that it? High up in the sand?"

His sharp eyes were right. It took Alan another five hundred paces before he could see the little red boat hauled above the tidemark.

Ches carefully placed Cathy under the awning and pushed the boat to the water's edge. Alan got in beside her, and Ches gave the boat a shove, jumping in before the water could touch his toes.

"Urr," he shuddered. "Nasty stuff. Whatever it is."

"Haven't you seen the sea before?"

"Once or twice," the Nuone said. "We're desert creatures. I hope none of that wet stuff gets in here. What do we do now? How do we make it move?"

With a start Alan remembered. He carefully placed Sparkie on the prow.

"Take us to Charlie," he said. "To the last island of the Diamond realm."

Chapter Twenty

NO LUCK FOR LUCKY

Lucky poured over several transparent sheaves covered with silvery writing. "Aha, Dulstar!"

Dulstar looked up from his parchments. "Yes, Princess?"

"It's coming back to me now. I did examine Thulian powers the time Goldie sought refuge in Nivram. Seemed to me that we would need knowledge of it, but it turned out otherwise for the Goldener people." She turned another page. "Yes, that makes sense." She looked up. "I can translate this into our own powers, assuming Thulian magic has not evolved since then."

Dulstar blinked. "We shall shortly find out, Princess."

They hurried down to the great entrance to the Diamond home. With eyes sharpened by pursuing records of Thulian magic, Lucky could clearly see the barrier: fibrous, thin and almost completely invisible. If the spoken spell did not demolish the barrier, she would have to construct a weapon to cut those threads, but it would take time. It had been three days since their unknown enemy had attacked. She did not want to spend another day finding a different means of breaking it. Weak from her exertions to heal her father, Lucky hoped she had enough strength for the counter spell.

The antechamber was quiet. The Diamonds who usually filled the outer chambers with sweet music had been called away, either to assist in the king's cure or to recover from this work. Lucky recited the words that would free them, focusing all her Diamond magic on the transparent curtain. It shook, it trembled, she could see the helix start to untangle but then hesitate. Lucky redoubled her efforts but in vain. The threads wound around each other even firmer than before.

"Did it work?" Dulstar asked once she had finished.

"No. At least this spell did not set off any booby-traps." It had been a risk, as the Thulians liked to punish others for interfering with their spells. "Give me a minute to find out what I did wrong, Dulstar." Summoning up her reserves, Lucky probed the curtain, to discover why it had resisted her magic.

She laughed.

"What is it, Princess?"

"Interesting. My spell is correct, Dulstar, but must be uttered from the exterior of the curtain, from the place where the original spell was cast. Clever."

"How can you get out to cast it from outside?"

"Unfortunately I can't." A gleam of sun broke through the clouds making the invisible curtain sparkle. Lucky turned away. "Back to work, Dulstar. We must proceed with plan two, a magical weapon to cut ourselves free. Whoever did this will be sorry they have made us go to so much effort," Lucky said as they left the chamber.

Chapter Twenty-one

ESCAPE

T remere sat back on the bed, arms behind his head, as if he
was still shackled, while Paul cracked open the door and
beckoned the porter to enter.

Lenno's unease spread across his features as Paul closed the
door.

"Your highness, is everything well?"

"Lenno, are you a man loyal to the crown?" Paul put on his
most serious expression.

"I'd give my life for you," Lenno said earnestly.

At last, a loyal subject. Paul nearly skipped for joy.

"I shall reward you greatly for your service," Paul declared.
"Can I trust you?"

Lenno nodded eagerly.

"I see that I can," the prince said. "Lenno, in recent months
our beloved kingdom has been in trouble, in upheaval."

"There has been...talk," Lenno said, glancing at Tremere.

"It's more than talk, I am afraid. I have uncovered a conspiracy against me, and against our country. Or enemies plan to destroy us."

Lenno inhaled sharply. "Oh, your highness, we feared as much. 'Take care of yourself up in the palace,' my wife is always saying to me. 'Trouble is coming'."

"She is a wise woman –"

"Wants me to retire from me job, she does," Lenno continued, plainly scared. "Says we'll make enough to live on from her little herb garden but that barely feeds the childer."

"You will be able to retire after you receive your reward for your assistance today. You shall all live in *comfort* for the rest of your days. How does that sound?" Would comfort be a good enough promise, Paul wondered. Should he have said *luxury*?

A beam broke across Lenno's face. "Sounds wonderful, your honour."

"But first you must help me. This gentleman holds the key to the conspiracy."

"Thought he looked dangerous the moment I clapped eyes on him," Lenno said.

"No, no." Paul took a deep breath. "He will help to end the conspiracy and prevent trouble from breaking out. He is on our side, a friend, who is unjustly held here." Lenno's smile faded, and he looked confused. Paul hastened into speech. "You have seen a small creature that goes about with our regent. Keeps himself covered, hidden under a long cloak?"

Lenno nodded.

"He is behind this innocent man's imprisonment. In order to save our country, I must get the prisoner out of the palace without Sylverine, that enemy in our midst, knowing about it."

"I hope you manage it, your highness." Lenno's face now carried an expression of extreme anxiety. "I do indeed."

"We will, with your help. I need you to exchange clothes with the prisoner. I shall get him past the guards by pretending he is the gate keeper." Paul looked a little doubtfully at Lenno. A good three inches shorter than Tremere, and probably fifty pounds heavier, it seemed unlikely the gatekeeper's blue uniform would pass muster on Tremere.

"How will you get past the gate?" Lenno sounded interested. "I called young Williams to stand in for me."

"Is he loyal?" Paul asked. "Can I trust him?"

"All your soldiers are loyal to you, your highness." Lenno cleared his throat, still keeping a wary eye on Tremere who had lowered his arms. "If you don't mind my saying so, your highness should not go out in the city. It's not safe."

"I shall be fine."

"I mean that with all your fine clothes you'll be recognised. The cry will go up that the prince is walking among the streets and the conspirators will be warned."

"Good point." Tremere clapped Lenno on the shoulder. "There'll be a bonus in that reward, won't there, Paul?"

"I have a cloak you could take. Inside the gate of the prison. My room there has a few things you might think useful," Lenno said.

"A double bonus," Paul said, feeling a wave of gratitude for this loyal subject. "Thank you, Lenno."

"One last thing, if I might make so bold, your highness." Lenno cleared his throat. "If I may ask, where might you be going? Will you be leaving the city? Pardon me for asking, your honour."

Paul's plan was to head back to Nivram as soon as possible and ask Lucky for help to save his kingdom.

"Weadle," he said, naming the village closest to the border with Nivram.

Lenno nodded, but looked puzzled. "Well, your honour, I mean your highness, that's a long walk and you best not try to take a carriage from the palace. But if I might suggest, my sister Sarah, her husband Hams, has a cart, and they'd be honoured to drive you there. Save you the walk and all."

Paul had been so focused on getting Tremere out of the dungeons that he hadn't thought much about the long walk back to Nivram. Lenno was due a wonderful reward for his service once Slithery was disposed of.

"Thank you, Lenno," he said, moved by the devotion of his subject. "I shall not forget."

The gatekeeper then swapped clothes with Tremere. The uniform was slightly short and rather too loose on Tremere, but Paul assured him that he looked fine. Lenno, on the other hand, could not close Tremere's shirt or trousers, and his grey undergarments were visible. Paul found a coarse blanket at the far end of the room, and gave it to him.

"Thank you, your highness. The boys would laugh at me otherwise when I return to me quarters."

"Laugh at you?" Tremere said. "You'll be a hero."

This made Lenno look much happier again.

"The guards check the prisoners frequently. They will free you soon," Paul said.

"Tell them I forced you to exchange clothes by holding a knife to the prince's throat," Tremere said.

"If you please, sir, tie me up or clobber me or something to stop me sounding the alarm," Lenno begged.

Tremere took the cord from his leather bag and bound Lenno's wrists and ankles. He put the end of the cord into Lenno's hand and told him that if he pulled it when the guards came, the knots would tighten convincingly.

Lenno then reminded him that he could call for help so Tremere tied Paul's handkerchief across this mouth.

"If you need a drink, you can push it aside. Don't forget to pull it back in place so you appear well gagged."

They left Lenno sitting upon the floor, looking quite happy. He was probably dreaming about his retirement. Paul hoped he would be able to keep his promise to the gatekeeper.

"Let me go first," Tremere said.

Paul shook his head. "I'll lead. If you are recognised, hold your knife to my throat and bargain your way out."

"Are you sure your soldiers love you that much?" Tremere said with a grin.

Paul frowned. "Ssh." He did not appreciate Tremere's humour.

Paul confidently led the way. Passing by the communal cells, the shouts and cries of the inmates did not upset him this time, as it meant Tremere went by unnoticed. The guards bowed as Paul passed, and never glanced at his companion. It looked like his escape plan was going to work.

They reached the prison gate unchallenged. The door to Lenno's room was ajar.

"In here first." Tremere pushed his way inside. A cloak hung on the back of the door, and a flagon of wine and a loaf of bread stood on the table. Tremere cut several slices of bread and ate them hastily.

"As you do not believe in feeding your prisoners, I am helping myself to the provisions." He also poured out a glass of wine and tossed it back. Paul looked for a weapon but found nothing.

"What do you know of this other guard, Williams?" Tremere said.

Paul shook his head, to indicate nothing.

"We shouldn't take any chances, not at this stage," Tremere said. "We are too close to escape, so allow me deal with this."

Paul stood back as Tremere opened the door on a young man standing with his back to them. Tremere threw an arm around his neck and pressed his knife against the man's stomach.

"Don't make a sound," Tremere said, quietly but with force.

The man did not resist as Tremere dragged him inside. Once Paul shut the door, Tremere moved his knife, reversed it, and hit the man on the head. Williams collapsed immediately.

"Not my preferred means of operating," Tremere said, dragging the body into the gatekeeper's room. "But at least he's unconscious for the next few minutes. I hope that's long enough for our purposes."

Williams wore a brown cloak over his uniform and carried a sword at his side. Tremere removed both items, and gave the cloak to Paul.

"I'll take Lenno's," he said, buckling on the sword belt.

Leaving the palace proved to be surprisingly easy. Paul felt a little disappointed that despite all Reece's extra guards, not one challenged the two hooded figures in the long brown cloaks.

A busy market was taking place in one of the larger squares. The plaza was crowded with stalls and penned livestock, and people had come from all over the country to barter their goods. Paul threaded his way through the crowds, his cloak kept tightly closed as he listened intently to snatches of conversation, hoping he would learn something of what was happening in his country. He half feared what he would discover, but he heard nothing of any value. Most people were concerned with the price of the produce, the quality of the foodstuff, and the difficulty of getting hold of meat. It was only as Paul exited the marketplace he overheard any talk of soldiers. An elderly man spoke of the constant harassing of folk in the city while his companion mentioned troops careering about the countryside doing the same.

"Any who object are thrown into jail," one said. "They say the palace dungeons are crowded."

"It's surely time for change," his friend said. "The people won't take much more of this."

Tremere urged Paul forward. "Keep going, that will keep."

Paul led Tremere to the city gate where a queue of people waited to exit. He couldn't tell if this was usual, for the royal household used a private entrance close to the palace. It made him uneasy, as if word had reached them already of Tremere's escape, but he said nothing as he shuffled along the line. Ahead, a man wearing a broad-brimmed hat was stopped and asked to remove it so that the guard could see his face. The man cheerfully obliged and was then waved through. Paul felt nervous as his turn came. Surely they would recognise him? Would the expensive fabric of his clothes beneath the rough cloak make the guard suspicious?

Paul was waved through immediately, for they had no interest in stopping boys. He stepped gladly through the arched gateway. Luckily, it was market day. Tremere's pale face would not stand out so much among all the strangers in the city.

"Hey! You! Stop!" A shout from a sentry made him look back. The guard held his spear in front of Tremere, blocking his way. "Trying to sneak past me, were you?"

"No," Tremere said, his voice altered to sound more like Lenno's accents. "Only on me road home."

"What will I tell the wife then?" the guard continued. "That her own brother won't pass the day's greeting with me."

Paul relaxed. A case of mistaken identity, that was all.

Tremere pushed back his hood to let his face be seen clearly. "Sadly, I'm not lucky enough to be your wife's brother."

The guard stared at him and then burst out laughing.

"Not ugly enough neither! The beard looked alike, that and your general size. Apologies, sir, for the mistake." He clapped Tremere on the shoulder and raised the spear.

"He did my heart no favours," Tremere said, re-joining Paul. "Where to from here?"

"Lenno's sister lives in the next village," Paul said. Beyond the bridge the main highway continued north while a narrow road led south-east. The village was marked on the signpost.

"Forty furlongs, a short stroll," Tremere said.

Paul thought otherwise but said nothing.

Chapter Twenty-two

SUSAN'S FRIEND

S usan gently stroked the head of the firebird which lay on her lap. It had taken many visits and much perseverance to build up this level of trust, but it was worth it. The firebird's head was large and heavy, several times the size of her own, but Susan stroked it as tenderly as if it were a small puppy. Golden feathers now sprouted thickly on its head, and they were wonderfully soft to the touch.

Ever since she had found a crack in her cell wall that she could squeeze through, she and the firebird had become friends. She was no longer required for fire-tending duties, which was also a relief. Susan had found the work backbreaking. In her new prison, the wardens visited exactly three times a day, at the same hour each day, so Susan slipped back into her own cell to be present when they brought her food and fresh water.

Once she had fallen asleep against her new friend's side, but the firebird had gently nudged her awake in time for her to get back to her own cell.

The only disadvantage of spending so much time with the firebird was that Susan would get terribly warm. The firebird emitted heat like a furnace, the soft feathers insulated it, and whenever the firebird opened her mouth, flames shot out.

The firebird never spoke, so Susan did all the talking. She told of her life in Lowdar, and the firebird stirred angrily at the mention of the bullies that used to torment Susan. A hot tear splashed on Susan's hand as she described the dark days between her parents' death and meeting Lucky.

"I shouldn't tell you only the gloomy things," Susan said. "When there is so much good. I have three wonderful sisters and a fantastic brother. Let me tell you about them."

The firebird pressed against her, as if to say it was happy to hear it, but beneath this Susan could sense the terrible loneliness of the creature. So Susan told the firebird about her family, and their adventures with Lucky. When she mentioned the first time she saw Queen Rose, the firebird shivered, and Susan could barely break the news about her own capture by the witch.

"If only I knew your name," Susan said, pushing a golden feather out of one blue eye.

The firebird sang softly under its breath, but Susan could not understand what it hummed.

"I'd love you to meet Vicky. She's caught down here too, but I haven't seen her since the first day. Maybe she has escaped." The guards told her Vicky had been assigned to work on another part of their tunnels, and they both would be free soon. Fear for Vicky's safety gnawed at Susan constantly but she was comforted by the thought that if anyone could escape, it would be Vicky. She pictured Lucky, her father, and Charlie flying in to rescue her and the firebird, but wished she had some way to rescue herself. Without her flute, she had no chance of escape. She missed it terribly but at least it was safe with Vicky. "Shall I tell you about my flute?"

The firebird, head in her lap, made a purring sound.

"My mother gave it to me, when she was dying. It plays the sweetest music in the world. The Diamonds call it the Lost Flute of Thule, but..." She broke off. At the mention of Thule, the firebird had become agitated. It raised its head and opened its mouth. Flames shot out, fortunately above Susan's head, though it singed a few strands of her hair. She gave a little cry as the firebird got to its feet, its head brushing against the ceiling as it breathed fire once more.

Then it stretched out its wings. Susan had only ever seen them snug against its body, barely noticeable. Now she saw how delicate they were, skeins of gold that looked insubstantial, but so large that they pushed against the wall as a shower of golden feathers fell gently to the floor.

As if realising that there was no room to fly, the firebird folded away its wings and looked sadly down at Susan, before settling down once more into its nest.

"I'm sorry," Susan said. For one split second she had felt over-awed and intimidated by the firebird. "I didn't mean to upset you. Do you know Thule?"

The firebird laid its head on her lap once more and gazed at her sorrowfully.

"I don't know anything about him," Susan said. "I guess Thule is a guardian too, like Lucky."

The firebird heaved a sigh. Steam shot out through its nostrils, but it kept its mouth closed.

"I had a strange dream earlier when I fell asleep beside you," Susan went on. "I dreamed I was in a great nest, high above the ground. The nest was made of gold but filled with lovely soft feathers, red and gold ones, like yours. Below me was a city encircled by a golden wall and full of funny triangular buildings, all pointing up towards me. If I fell on them, I thought I should be pierced to the heart. The city was perched on an island in the middle of a golden lake. Surrounding the lake was a vast desert, row upon row of dunes were thrown up out of the sand like angry waves on the sea." The firebird settled its head a little deeper on her lap. "Somewhere among the dunes a great beast awaited me. I knew its eyes were fixed upon me, and I had the feeling that if I moved, it would launch an attack against me."

Susan's light blue eyes met the firebird's dark blue ones in a flash of comprehension.

"That's *your* dream, isn't it?" Susan whispered. "No, it's more than a dream, it's where you live." She bent over and hugged as much of the creature's head and neck as she could, until her face grew red from the heat and she had to straighten up. "I'm sorry, firebird." She stroked it again.

If she dreamed of the firebird's life, would the firebird dream of hers? She hoped the firebird picked up on her happy recent memories, lying in the sunshine beside Crocodile Lake and chatting to Lucky and Charlie, and not life in Lowdar. Or worse...being held captive in Queen Rose's pyramid castle, helplessly watching her torture other creatures and laughingly warning Susan, *You'll be next.*

Chapter Twenty-three

RETURN TO MOUNT SLANT

The journey back to the last island of the Diamond realm proved worse than that out to Thule. The sun seemed to burn with an even greater zest, and while Ches revelled in it, lying flat on the base of the boat and enjoying every ray, Alan crouched under the awning beside Cathy, bathing her forehead with seawater. Every now and again he gazed towards the prow of the boat to check that Sparkie was still there, before glancing at Ches to see if he had moved. Then back to Cathy, trying to cool her down, and frequently wetting her lips from the diminishing supply of drinking water.

This time he would make sure Ches did not get hold of what was left in the water bottle.

After a while Alan fell into an uneasy doze. When he woke the sea was reflecting the golds and pinks of a glorious sunset. The last island appeared ahead. No sign of Charlie but Alan was certain his friend would be waiting for their return, as he had promised.

Ches was sitting up and looking unhappy. The sun's rays were still warm, but the sea breeze was making itself felt more strongly in the weakening sunlight.

"I'm getting cool," he said, fixing his yellow eyes first on Sparkie before shifting his gaze onto Alan. "Soon I shall be cold and die. You must keep your promise."

"We're almost there." Alan pointed to the island where the golden beach disappeared into the green hills. "Look."

"There's something wrong," Ches said. "The colour is not right."

He seemed anxious.

"It's green. Grass and bushes and flowers grow there. Haven't you seen them before?" It hadn't occurred to Alan that Ches had known nothing but the desert.

"I like the desert. Sand like gold, sun like gold, heat like gold." Ches shivered and looked longingly towards Sparkie.

Alan much preferred the lush grass and cooler clime of Nivram to the horrible heat of the desert. He turned back to Cathy, tossing restlessly, and gently dribbled some seawater onto her forehead, hoping to cool her down.

Charlie was asleep when they almost ran into him, bobbing gently just off a sheltered cove. Alan's shout of greeting roused him in time to dodge the boat. Sparkie had taken Alan's instruction literally.

"Whoa! I know you're glad to see me but that's ridiculous," Charlie said. Charlie took in Cathy lying prone under the awning, and he glanced sharply at Ches. However, his beam of welcome did not fade. "Let's get you to shore."

Alan introduced Ches to Charlie as he jumped out into the shallows and helped shove the little boat up to dry sand.

"A canoe?" Ches sounded suspicious. "I've never heard of canoes. But then I never heard of humans before these two turned up."

"He's a Diamond really," Alan said. "Sometimes he takes the form of a canoe."

"Oh, Diamonds," Ches said. "I've heard of them." His tone implied he had heard nothing good of Diamonds.

"We Diamonds are all familiar with tales from Thule," Charlie said. "Though I don't believe I've ever met a Nuone before. Met Thulians."

"Possibly those that left before the Great Trouble. If they had stayed, perhaps they could have prevented it," Ches said sourly. He picked up Cathy and stepped onto the sand.

"The Nuones wouldn't be in charge of Thule now, if that had been the case, would they?" Charlie cocked a curious eyebrow at Ches.

"Put that way, I'm grateful to them. Where do you want the girl?" Ches said.

"What happened?" Charlie sounded concerned and his normally cheerful expression was absent.

"A giant snake bit her as we escaped the city," Alan said, his relief at reaching the island almost overwhelming him. Charlie would know what to do to cure Cathy.

"So you didn't get such a good welcome, after all? Take her to the back of the beach, there's a sheltered area at the foot of the hills. Then gather some firewood," Charlie said.

Ches reluctantly accompanied Alan to collect driftwood while Charlie examined Cathy's wound.

Arriving back with a heavy armload of wood, Alan noticed Charlie looked unusually serious. He dropped his bundle. "What?"

"It's bad, Alan," Charlie said. "The snake's bite was poisonous."

Ches had already told him that. Alan waited to hear how soon Charlie could cure her.

"Can't you fix her either?" Ches came up behind Alan. "I thought Diamonds were healers."

"Some of us are. I'm not. Alan, come over here for a moment." Charlie led Alan out of earshot from Ches. "Is this creature going to help us?"

"He promised he'd free the Diamonds."

"Do you trust him?"

Alan wasn't sure. "Sometimes."

"Enough to take him back with us?" Charlie said. "I don't want to carry any unnecessary weight. Where did you meet him?"

"In a dungeon," Alan said. "He's our only chance to break the Thulian spell. He helped us escape the Nuones."

"In a...? Never mind, tell me later. We need to get back to the Rock as soon as possible. Lucky will cure Cathy. Don't worry, we've time. But we should go now."

Alan was sick with disappointment. Now Cathy would have to wait for many more hours before getting help, and what if Ches couldn't free the Diamonds?

"All right. Oh, here's your chip back, thank you. It saved our lives. Ches's too."

"I hope he's grateful," Charlie said. "Keep the chip for the moment, Alan, until we get home."

Ches looked at them in amazement when he heard the news.

"You mean I've been breaking my back collecting wood for you, and now we are not going to use it? Instead we are to sail across the cold sea while the night freezes the life from my limbs? I'm not going."

"I'll give you Sparkie to keep you warm," Alan said.

"Very well." Ches sighed. "I don't like this place anyway. I suppose you want me to carry her back to the boat?"

"I'll take us back, we'll be faster," Charlie said. "If you would place her inside my interior...thank you. Now down to the shore, you two can hop in once we get there. I prefer not to carry you further than I have to."

Despite everything, it was good to be back in Charlie. Ches cheered up once Sparkie was again pinned to his tunic. Even Cathy looked more relaxed in Charlie's cushioned interior.

Alan intended to stay awake to watch over Cathy, but he soon fell asleep.

He woke as the day began to break. Ches was happily asleep in a bubble of warmth while Cathy slept peacefully beside Alan. The sea, grey and cold-looking, stretched in every direction.

"How far?" he said to Charlie, raising his voice

Charlie struggled to answer as he was buffeted by waves, but Alan managed to catch his reply. "Another couple of hours and we'll reach land."

Then there would be another half a day at least of flight before they reached Mount Slant. Alan sat close to Cathy and told her soon they'd be back home and Lucky would make her better. His eye fell on Ches, fiddling with Sparkie. He had no idea what Ches would do. Would the Nuone keep his promise, or had he some other agenda in mind?

Chapter Twenty-four

THE ROCK

The familiar crooked shape of Mount Slant appeared in the distance, with the shimmer of blue at its base. Alan gave a cheer. He grabbed Cathy's hand and squeezed it.

"Yippee! We're almost home."

Ches sniffed. "Hurrah for you."

Alan ignored him. He had grown tired of Ches and his constant complaints. First the sea was too dangerous and death by waves was imminent. When Charlie flew, Ches complained the clouds looked sinister so Alan explained what they were. Ches had never heard of anything so terrifying, water falling from the sky, that horrible stuff in Alan's flask nearly killed him! He wanted Charlie to turn around and go straight back to Thule.

However, Charlie didn't listen, so Ches, keeping Sparkie close to his heart, looked sulky, and complained about the speed and height that they were flying at, the cold breeze that caused him to suffer, and the lack of anything decent to drink, such as the oily substance Alan had seen him quaff in Thule.

"I hope it rains. Soon," Alan said.

Ches threw him a hurt and offended glance, and turned away.

"We're out of water," Alan said. He hadn't said it to be mean. "Cathy needs it, and so do I."

Cathy's wound had blackened, her brow shone with fever, and she moved restlessly in her sleep. Yet the closer they got to Mount Slant, the more Alan's hopes rose that Lucky would soon cure her, and Cathy would be sitting up laughing and chattering, telling exaggerated tales of her few moments in Fang's mouth. He wouldn't consider anything else happening.

The waters of Crocodile Lake gleamed in the sun and Charlie flew lower and landed with a slight thump.

"Ouch," Ches complained, though Alan had barely felt it.

"If you two could alight," Charlie said, "I will bring Cathy up to the Rock. Alan, you lead the way."

The canoe sounded tired. Alan didn't understand why Charlie didn't land on the plateau outside the Diamond entrance but there was probably some silly rule about it.

"Sure," he said, hopping out, enjoying the feel of the solid ground beneath his feet, the sweet scent of flowers, and that indefinable smell he detected from Crocodile Lake. It felt like home. His spirits rose as he started up the rocky path. Ches followed, muttering to himself, while Charlie, lumbering awkwardly on his four feet, brought up the rear.

The slope was steep, and Alan was panting hard by the time he reached the entrance to the Rock of Diamonds. The large arch, dark this time, shrank as Alan approached it.

"So this is the famous Rock of Diamonds." Ches came up quietly behind Alan, taking the climb in his stride. He gazed at the entrance for a few moments. "It's Thulian magic all right. Side two though. We Nuones never got past side one. Few of us even got to side one."

"What do you mean?" Alan said sharply. Ches *had* to break the spell. "You said you have Thulian blood. You freed us."

"The lower points, like those for locking and unlocking doors, are not Thulian magic. They're simple Nuone tricks. Nothing to them. The first level of Thulian powers is base. From there the advanced ones go to side one, that's where Anea, Barne, and those like me are." Ches turned away to stare at the magnificent view that lay before him. He waved a scrawny paw towards the fields and the lake. "Kind of ugly, isn't it?"

"How many sides are there?" Alan said, paying no attention to Ches's comment.

"Three sides. And then the apex. That's where the Thulians went wrong. The Apex is forbidden to all but Thule. That's why they were punished." He turned back and his strange eyes looked sideways at Alan. "Nuones cannot, under any circumstances, progress past side one."

"I don't care what the rules are," Alan said, snatching the sliver of Diamond from Ches's tunic and jumping back out of reach. "You break that spell or you'll die here tonight."

Ches's eyes burned yellow as he glared at Alan, who braced himself. Ches could easily wrest Sparkie out of his hand, Alan knew, but it would do Ches no good, for Alan controlled the chip. The same realisation seemed to cross Ches's mind, for the fire died out in his eyes and they resumed their usual pale colour, and his voice when he spoke was calm.

"You know, of course, that I could lift you over the edge of the cliff and shake you until you swore to keep me alive tonight. Of course, you already promised to do that. I didn't think you would break your word."

"*You* promised to break the Thulian spell," Alan said.

"Very well. I will try. Should I fail, remember I did my best."

Charlie came puffing around the corner of the path. "Ches is ready to start," Alan said, relieved his bluff had not been called.

Charlie sat down, his feet tucked by his side. "Go ahead."

Ches stepped in front of the archway, but at a distance so that the arch was almost his height. Muttering a stream of words, Ches swayed from side to side, his hands moving rapidly, as if he was forming pictures or shapes with his claws. Alan couldn't tell if he was really working to break the spell or putting on a performance to save his life.

Whichever it was, Ches was visibly tiring. The faint colour of his cheeks completely faded, he grew breathless, and a dark substance began to congeal on his brow.

"Nothing's happening," Alan whispered.

"Give him time," Charlie said.

Ches fell silent, but his arm movements continued. Then, like a flash, he stood on his head, both hands and feet continuing to carve elaborate movements in the air.

The sound of shattering glass broke the silence. A thousand fragments of the broken spell shot out into the air and dissolved, while Ches fell over on the ground.

Chapter Twenty-five

THE SPELL IS BROKEN

Alan ducked instinctively. When he looked up, Ches was curled into a ball, arms around his head.

"Well done, well done," Charlie said, stamping his feet on the ground in applause.

"Is it really broken?" Alan said, unable to believe his eyes.

"Yes," Charlie said. "It's over."

Cathy lay unconscious in Charlie's interior, her colour risen once more, the poison spreading throughout her body.

"Please go and get Lucky, Charlie," Alan begged.

Charlie hesitated. "Better if I stay here with Cathy. Lucky will come out once she learns the spell is broken. Are you all right, Ches?"

Ches groaned and unwrapped his head to look up. "Did I really do it? You owe me, boy. That was the hardest thing I ever had to do." He staggered to his feet.

"That was good," Alan said. A sparkle of light caught his attention. Lucky had already emerged from the Rock. "Lucky! Cathy's really sick, you *have* to cure her."

"Where is she?" Lucky said immediately.

"I have her," Charlie said.

There was a flash as Lucky hopped onto Charlie, and looked at Cathy. "What happened? What's wrong with her?"

"The serpent protector of Thule poisoned her," Ches said.

Lucky glowed briefly but kept her attention on Cathy. "So you did go to Thule, then. All of you?" She hopped down beside the sick girl.

"Not exactly," Charlie said, surprisingly evasive.

"Only Cathy and I went," Alan said.

"And a little part of me," Charlie added.

"Oh, Charlie." Lucky sighed. She appeared once more at Charlie's prow.

"Is she better yet?" Alan asked anxiously. He hadn't seen any magic spark fly from Lucky.

"My father was injured endeavouring to break the Thulian enchantment. He is recovering slowly. I've spent three days in the healing chamber. My reserves are very low."

"What do you mean?" Alan didn't like the way Lucky was talking.

"If Cathy had a cold, broken her leg, or any normal injury, I could cure her immediately. So could Charlie. But an illness caused by magic... and the serpent Thule left to watch over the Nuones is an enchanted beast... takes huge effort to cure. Thulian magic is particularly difficult."

"What about the healing chamber?" Charlie said. "Could some of the other Diamonds help?"

"No. Impossible to get her in there. I can make her comfortable for the moment, and later, when I am stronger, try to rid her of the poison."

"Is there time?" Charlie asked Lucky. "It's been almost two days."

"I don't know."

The shock of Lucky's words left Alan numb. He had been so sure that Lucky would take one look and be able to cure Cathy.

Ches spoke up. "I can help."

Alan glared at him. "You can cure her? Why didn't you say so before?"

"Nobody asked," Ches said. "All I can do is withdraw the poison, which will leave her desperately weak. Can you give her the energy to survive?"

"Yes," Lucky said. "Thank you."

Ches nodded. "You get kind of fond of someone you have to lug about the place." Stepping close to Charlie, he gently lifted up Cathy. Placing her on the ground, he exposed her stomach wound and laid a claw over it. Then he began to sing tunelessly but loudly while Alan anxiously watched.

The infection had spread across Cathy's stomach, turning it an ugly mix of septic green and poisonous black. A putrid smell rose from it, as if Cathy's flesh were rotting. As Ches sang, the spread of infection shrank, and the smell faded. The wound began to contract and her flesh returned to normal. Soon the lesion had shrunk to half its size, and slowly disappeared beneath the claw, which turned a dark green as if Ches were sucking the poison up though his arm. Finally the singing stopped, Ches got up, walked over to the edge of the cliff and spat. Alan didn't see what fell but he did notice that Ches's arm had resumed its usual pale colour when he returned to Cathy's side.

Cathy looked deadly pale but the fever was gone.

"Quick!" Ches barked. "You're losing her."

A rain of sparks flew from Lucky and settled on Cathy's eyes, her mouth, her stomach and even her feet. The deathly pallor left her cheeks, Alan could see her breath again, and a few moments later she opened her eyes.

"I'm hungry," she said.

Charlie chuckled. "You sound just like your twin."

"Hey," Alan said, trying to hide his relief. "About time you came back to us." He held Cathy's arm and helped her to her feet. "Are you all right?"

"Starving," Cathy said. "Tired too. How did we get here? The last thing I remember..." She shuddered. "I was nearly eaten. Yuk! His breath stank. What happened?"

"Tell you later. Thanks, Lucky," Alan said.

Lucky nodded to Ches. "It's your friend here you should thank, whoever he is."

A wave of gratitude for Ches swept over Alan, and he repented of all the times he had doubted the Nuone. "If I could, I'd give you the chip," he said, "but it's not mine."

"You saved me, Ches, did you?" Cathy said happily.

"*Twice*," Ches said.

"Did you also break the Thulian curse?" Lucky said. "How did you do that?"

"I'm Nuone. With a little bit of Thulian in me," Ches muttered. "I know the first step of Thulian."

"That was of the second side," Lucky said.

Ches obviously knew more Thulian magic than he wanted to admit to, but Lucky's voice was friendly. Alan could detect no sign in her words of the suspicion he felt.

"Nuones are not allowed to know any more... but I am impressed by your knowledge," Ches said.

"Lucky knows everything," Cathy said.

"We need to get you food and rest," Charlie said anxiously. "Lucky, Yvonne is trapped in the cottage and she's not the only one sealed into their home."

Lucky shone brighter at Charlie's words. "Perhaps Ches would be kind enough to break a few more of those spells?"

Ches nodded his agreement and they set off down the path.

"Yvonne will be so happy to see us," Cathy said, smiling happily. She looked pale and tired but otherwise herself, so Alan put aside his suspicions of Ches for the moment.

"She'll be more than happy," Charlie said.

Charlie was right. The children's home was the first cottage Ches unsealed and Yvonne fell upon the twins, hugging them tightly.

"I was so worried about you," she said. "I knew you'd be safe with Charlie but you were gone so long."

"We had to cross to the other side of the world and kidnap a creature from another species, rescue the Diamonds, and save Cathy from a poisonous snake," Alan said, struggling free of her embrace.

"Ha, ha," Yvonne said. "At least you weren't stuck inside with me, afraid to light the fire in case the chimney was blocked. No heat, and no warm food."

"It's *true*," Cathy said. "I'm back from the dead, and I am starving."

Chapter Twenty-six

CHARLIE IN TROUBLE

After lunch, Alan led the way back to the Rock. Yvonne had taken the story of their adventures in Thule far better than he expected, but the news of Susan and Vicky's disappearance had shocked her.

Charlie and Ches were sitting outside the entrance when they arrived, waiting for Lucky who was checking on her father.

Yvonne glanced briefly at Ches but focused on Charlie. "Oh Charlie, what about Susan and Vicky? Where are they?"

"Don't worry, Yvonne," Charlie said. "We'll get them back, safe and sound. Cathy, you look tired, would you like to sit in?"

"Yes, please. Thank you, Charlie." Cathy scrambled inside the canoe.

Now that they were safely back in Nivram, Alan knew the time had come to return Sparkie. Owning a magical item was something he dreamed of for as long as he could remember. Sparkie had made him forget the pain of not having one when all his sisters did. But Sparkie was not merely a thing of magic but a part of Charlie, and, despite Alan's reluctance, had to be returned.

"Charlie, I still have your chip. Here it is." Alan held out the sliver of Diamond which sparkled in the sunlight. "Ches will need it when the sun goes down though. Or else a very large fire."

"So it was your magic all along," Ches said, his eyes darting from Alan to Charlie. "I thought it was the boy's."

"Don't worry about Ches, Alan," Charlie said. "Lucky is fetching him a chip of his own."

Alan was glad to hear it. He didn't want Ches to suffer the torments of cold at night.

"One that will keep me nice and warm," Ches said. "Not one that is full of Diamond magic." He sounded regretful, as if he wished he had known at the time.

"I can't take it back, yet," Charlie said. "You hang on to it for the moment, Alan."

Alan was delighted to hold onto Sparkie for a little longer.

"But haven't you put all your magic into it?" Alan said. He slipped the chip into his pocket and silently told Sparkie to remain safely in his pocket.

"Yes," the canoe said.

"An extremely dangerous thing to do," Ches said. "You never know whose clutches it might fall into."

"I'll take good care of it, Charlie," Alan promised.

"You do that," Charlie said with a smile.

"You might have it longer than you think, boy," Ches said. "Your friend here has broken one of the most important rules of Diamond life, separating his powers from his body."

Charlie looked annoyed. "You really shouldn't eavesdrop, Ches."

"Sometimes it's helpful," the Nuone said, scratching his head.

"Are you in trouble, Charlie?" Alan said, concerned. Ches made it sound serious.

"Not for the first time." Charlie winked.

Alan knew this was true, but Charlie was sure to get back into the king's good graces again, especially as he was due to marry Lucky soon.

The late afternoon warmed the rock as it lowered behind the mountains separating east and west Nivram. Beyond the mountains lay the Great Forest. Alan longed to venture back into the forest, to go deep among the trees and fight the beasts that lurked there. With Sparkie's magic, he was sure he would succeed.

"Sorry for delaying you." Lucky appeared at the entrance to the Rock. "Current, Oak, come forward." Two Nilkens stepped into view. They must have been waiting silently at the top of the path to be called.

"Everything well?" Charlie asked as Lucky came to rest upon his prow.

"My father is doing better," Lucky said. "As to that other matter, I have no good news to report."

"I was afraid of that," Charlie said, looking glum.

"Now that we are all here, let us put together what we know," Lucky said in a clear silvery voice. "I recognised the magical trap that sealed the Rock to be Thulian, but other than that, I know nothing of this attack."

"Same with me," Yvonne said. "I was trapped in our cottage, and couldn't leave. I saw nothing strange beforehand."

"You had the same experience, didn't you, Oak?" Lucky turned to one of the Nilkens.

"Yes, Princess." Alan recognised Oak as one of the younger Nilkens who often brought food to the cottage. "All Nilken homes by Mount Slant were attacked in the same manner. By chance, most of us were inside at the time. Current was not."

"What happened to you, Current?" Charlie asked the other Nilken.

Current blushed, stepped forward and looked at his feet. "I escorted Prince Paul and your uncle, Tremere, over the Little Hills." Current spoke in a singsong manner. "After I returned, I reported to protection duty on the pathway."

"We never saw you." Alan remembered being struck by the absence of any Nilken guards as he and Cathy had climbed the path to the Rock.

"Jasmine and I were on duty when she disappeared before my eyes. Before I had time to cry out her name, a thick grey blanket engulfed me. I was helpless, unable to move, see or hear." Current looked distinctly unhappy with his experience. "Being close to the cliff edge, I was afraid of falling or of causing Jasmine to fall, so I stayed put."

Cathy gasped. "Did Jasmine fall? Is she all right?"

"It was a long way down," Current said.

Alan didn't know what to say. It seemed so horrible to think of the poor Milken crashing down the hill. He hoped that neither he nor Cathy had bumped into her on their way up the path that day.

"She is recovering and will be fine," Lucky said. "Ches, are you familiar with this magic?"

Ches cleared his throat. "Yes. It's first side. Only for advanced Nuones. Easy for skilled users of Thulian magic, Thulians, I mean."

"How does it work?" Alan was curious.

"A great invisible net. Engulfs you in a bubble. You can't see out, no one can see in, nobody notices you're there. More advanced than the base level on cottages, anyone could crack them. Not as powerful as the side two spell, which sealed the cavern behind us." Ches nodded towards the Diamond archway. "Whoever cast those didn't want to waste the time and effort that a second side spell would take. They saved *that* for the Diamonds."

"Susan and Vicky disappeared in front of us," Cathy said excitedly. "They must be stuck in that bubble stuff."

"Possibly," Lucky said. "But Ches has released all those trapped in these bubbles."

"How do you know?" Alan said. "If they're invisible."

"Not to me," Ches said. "Where did you last see your sisters?"

"We were coming up from the lake." Alan pointed in the general direction of the place where Susan and Vicky had disappeared. "They weren't far ahead of us."

Ches got up and walked over beside him. "You mean, near those trees, where the land rolls down to the shore? Those bubbles are giant spheres, not impervious to gravity."

"What do you mean?" Alan didn't like what Ches was implying.

"The answer is before you, boy. I didn't see them when I covered that ground, so they obviously rolled down the slopes and into the lake."

"I don't believe you." Annoyed by Ches's callous suggestion, Alan walked away from the edge and sat down beside Charlie.

"Both girls carry items with Thulian powers," Lucky said sharply. "I doubt very much if either of them fell into the lake."

"Really?" Ches sounded extremely interested. "What items would those be?"

Lucky ignored his question. "I believe whoever attacked us also took Vicky and Susan with them, probably *because* of their gifts. The questions we need to answer are: one, who is responsible for this attack. And two, what wicked plan do they have?"

Chapter Twenty-seven

SUSPICIONS

E veryone looked at Ches.

"What?" he said. "What did I do? Nothing. Except help those two escape from prison. Oh, and save Cathy's life. Twice. Wait a minute, I also freed the Diamonds from their chasm and these little people from their homes. Anyone once trapped in a bubble may also thank me."

"We're not accusing you, Ches," Charlie said calmly. "We're hoping you can help us."

"Everything points to Thule," Lucky said. "The spells cast are all Thulian magic. The only enemy we have is Witch Rose, a Thulian."

"Who is Witch Rose?" Ches said. "The name is not familiar."

"A member of the Thulian race, banished along with the others by Thule. Her Thulian name was Abcadarniz. She has a hatred of Diamonds, and regularly comes up with schemes to annoy us," Lucky said. "Only recently she hatched another plan against us, which failed. She hates us now more than ever."

Alan, watching Ches closely, thought he saw a gleam of recognition when Lucky mentioned her enemy's real name. He looked to Cathy to see if she had noticed but Cathy was curled up inside Charlie's warm interior, and fast asleep.

"The king banished her for a thousand years," Charlie said. "She cannot set foot in Nivram again until that time has elapsed."

"Abcadarniz." Ches let the name roll off his tongue. "No, I don't recall it. It is not familiar to me."

Neither Charlie nor Lucky gave any sign that they had noticed Ches's reaction.

"I believe she must be behind it, employing others to do her dirty work," Lucky said. "I can think of no-one else who would attack us. Tell me, Ches, do Nuones travel much?"

"No. Nuones prefer to stay in their golden city in the sun. We need safety and security, and much desert heat."

"What about that Nuone you mentioned?" Alan tried to recall what exactly Ches had muttered in their prison. "I can't remember his name, but he was low down in the system, and trouble."

"I have no idea of what you are talking about."

"Yes, you do," Alan said. "You thought he stole the firebird."

"I suppose you mean Sylverine," Ches said after a moment. "He is of the nineteenth order."

"The firebird?" Lucky sparkled with interest at Alan's words.

After a moment's hesitation, Ches related the story of the firebird's disappearance and how Fang was destroying his city.

"We'll help you save your city, if you help us," Lucky said.

Ches paced up and down for a few minutes before answering.

"Will you give me your word?" he asked.

"Yes. We will restore the firebird, or if that is not possible, we will fight and defeat Fang. You have my promise."

"Then I shall help you find your friends and destroy your enemy. I give you my word of honour." The way Ches stood tall as he spoke made him look noble.

"I know the word of honour of a Nuone, like that of a Thulian, is totally trustworthy," Lucky said quietly.

Ches nodded, back to his normal self. "You are right."

"I don't understand," Yvonne burst in. "How does this help Vicky and Susan? Can we find them instead of talking about it?"

Ches made a hoarse throaty sound. Laughing again. "There will be plenty of action ahead, don't worry."

"Why would Sylverine steal the firebird?" Charlie said. "That puzzles me."

"I think I can answer that," Alan said. Several pairs of eyes fixed on him in surprise. "It's obvious, isn't it? To keep himself and the Nuones with him warm at night."

Ches nodded. "That is certainly an important reason, and perhaps the only one. Sylverine would not care about those left behind to Fang. Indeed, he would be happy to learn of the other Nuones' destruction."

"Why is that, Ches?" Lucky shone a little brighter as she spoke.

"Anea and the other masters demoted him. Sylverine hates them."

"What order did he belong to originally?" Lucky said.

"He called himself Arrio. He was of the highest order prior to his demotion, he would know of much Thulian magic," Ches said. "You can take it that he planned the attack on your homes."

It had taken Ches a long time to provide so much information. Alan thought it strange that he suddenly was so open. Maybe it had taken Lucky's promise of assistance to make him helpful? Something nagged at the back of Alan's mind. Something that happened in Thule. He wished Cathy were awake, she would remember.

With this news, Lucky and Charlie talked quietly together, but Alan was close enough to overhear.

"The attack on the Rock was to stop us from finding out what they are up to," Charlie said.

"Which means whatever they are doing is taking place close enough to us that we would otherwise stumble upon it. Capturing Vicky and Susan must have been a bonus for Witch Rose." Lucky shot a look towards Alan as she said this, so he hastily looked away.

"Ches, what can the firebird do?" Lucky asked.

The Nuone thought carefully for a moment. "The firebird protects us from Fang, warms the night chamber, and draws the heat of the sun upon our city. Its feathers turn our lake gold. And it sings."

"Sings?" Charlie said.

"Very sweetly," Ches said. "I can't think of anything else Sylverine would want it for, except maybe turn the waters of your lake down there to gold." He chortled for the third time.

"I wonder," Lucky said.

Ches's jaw dropped. "That was a joke. It would be a great gift to you, not a punishment, if the firebird did so."

"The guardians of the world live below the waters of the lake," Lucky said. "Perhaps if the waters changed to gold, the guardians would wake."

"They would be turned to gold," Ches said. "Like everything that touches our golden lake. Except Fang."

"When the guardians wake, our tenure of protection over these lands is over," Lucky said. "Witch Rose may think turning the lake to gold would end Diamond power. Perhaps it would. But probably the whole world too, including herself."

Lucky's words were sombre. Despite the sunshine Alan felt cold. He met Yvonne's eyes and she smiled reassuringly at him.

"Our lake is small compared to yours," Ches said. "Turning that..." He nodded towards the expanse of blue water below. "...to gold would be beyond the powers of the firebird."

"How can you be sure?" Lucky said.

"Held captive, the firebird would be too miserable to grow golden feathers," Ches said. "When the firebird is troubled, the feathers change colour. I have seen red and white and sometimes no feathers at all. If that happens, the golden content of the lake drops, and Fang enters. Occasionally the masters devise a crazy plan, and only when they abandon it do the golden feathers return. Thule is thus controlling our behaviour, rewarding us when we are good, punishing us for any evil."

"Or protecting you, perhaps," Lucky said.

"Perhaps," Ches said. "Yes, you are right, protecting us. I am sorry. My drop of Thulian blood occasionally emerges. They were always set upon rebellion."

A Nilken appeared at the top of the rocky stair and bowed low.

"Your highness, a party approaches and wishes to speak to you."

Alan expected a delegation from Queen Rose, or perhaps even the evil Nuone Sylverine, to round the corner. Tremere and Paul were a surprise, especially Paul, who looked tired and unkempt.

"Here you all are." Paul sounded pleased. Then he gave a start. "Who's that?"

"This is Ches," Alan said. Tremere would be a great addition to the fight against Queen Rose. He was less sure about the prince. "A friend of ours from Thule. What are you doing back so soon?"

Cathy woke up amid all the noise of greeting. "Tremere," she shrieked in delight. "Hurrah! You're back." She climbed out of Charlie and ran over to her uncle. "I nearly died, twice. We went to Thule to rescue Vicky and Susan but instead we met Ches. He's going to help us battle Queen Rose."

"Queen Rose?" Paul said.

"Vicky and Susan?" Tremere said.

"Sit down," Lucky said. "I shall tell you what has been happening here."

Cathy resumed her comfortable spot in Charlie's bow. Paul got in beside her, asking Charlie's permission first, and Alan overheard him say, "Wait until you hear how I rescued your uncle."

Lucky gave the new arrivals a summary of events to date.

"Sylverine?" Tremere nodded at Ches. "Looks like him?"

Ches made a slight bow. "We are of the same species, Nuones."

"Sylverine has turned my regent against me, and against the Diamonds," Paul said. "Reece now thinks you are planning to attack Kyle. She believes Tremere spies for you, and she threw him into the dungeons for kidnapping me."

"Perhaps you better tell your story from the beginning," Lucky said.

Paul plunged into the tale, Tremere occasionally adding his piece.

"This is getting more and more complicated," Charlie said when Paul had concluded with their walk up the gorge. "Could the rogue Nuones be in Kyle, and not in Witch Rose's castle?"

Ches coughed for attention. "It's likely that Sylverine is distracting your neighbours as he did your kind, though in a different way."

"So you think Paul's country has no part in her plan?" Lucky said.

Ches smiled slowly. "I think not. I would like a few words with Sylverine. Perhaps if I travelled to this young man's palace, I could have a chat with him, and find out what this is all about. In the meantime, you could search around these slopes and the lake for any sign of your missing friends. Be vigilant though, in case the attackers return."

"I could fly you to the palace," Charlie said. "Much the quickest way of getting there."

"Thank you." Ches bowed but Alan could tell he had no intention of accepting Charlie's offer.

"What about that black bog in the valley over the hills?" Tremere said.

"The witch's castle burned the ground badly there. No doubt she left a residue of evil," Lucky said.

"This place seemed more than that," Tremere said with a frown. "As if it wanted to pull you into its depths. It almost got Paul."

"Just the sort of present Witch Rose would leave behind," Charlie said. "A lasting memorial to her evil ways."

Lucky looked to Ches. "What do you think?"

Ches shrugged. "An evil bog. Nothing more to it. Nothing Thulian, anyway."

"It's getting late," Lucky said. Gold and pink tinged the western sky. "I will speak to my father, about this and other things. I must also collect a small gift for Ches. When I return, we shall make our plans."

Current jumped to his feet. "I shall go and prepare an evening repast for our guests."

"You can stay with us, Ches," Alan said, torn between gratitude and suspicion.

Ches's eyes flickered over to him. "Thank you. How kind. Are you sure you have room for me?"

"We have room for everybody," Yvonne said warmly.

Lucky returned, and a small spark flew across to Ches's tunic, where it fastened itself and shone like a star.

"That should keep you warm at night while you remain with us," she said.

Ches stroked it with one claw. "I am grateful. Will it keep me warm at night in the desert also?"

"Yes," Lucky said.

"Then I am doubly grateful. The warming chamber gets so crowded."

"I talked to the king," Lucky said. "He is mulling over our approach, but it will be some time before he reaches a decision. Therefore, I suggest we meet here after breakfast."

Lucky's lack of urgency to rescue his sisters came as a surprise. Alan hoped she had a master plan she wasn't sharing, because otherwise it would be up to him. His plan at the moment was to watch Ches closely.

Yvonne looked disappointed. "What about my sisters?"

"They have waited so long already, another few hours will make little difference," Lucky said.

"Better to get our plans right first," Charlie said. "Don't worry, Yvonne. We'll have them back soon."

Yvonne was clearly unhappy, but she got to her feet, ready to return to the cottage. Tremere spoke to Alan and Yvonne in a low voice. "I will talk to Lucky and see what I can do."

Cathy had fallen asleep once more. Ches reached out to pick her up but Tremere stopped him. "I can take her."

"My day is getting better and better," Ches said, standing back. "She weighs a bit, I warn you."

"I can manage," Tremere said firmly, and bent to pick her up.

"Wake her up," Alan said as he followed Tremere down the slope. "I bet she is heavy." He wanted to talk to her, but she did not stir.

"She's fine," Tremere grunted.

In the cottage Cathy was put straight to bed while the rest of the company sat down to supper. It was a quiet meal, the diners weighed down by their thoughts. Despite Yvonne's talk, there was a shortage of beds in the cottage, so Tremere left with Current, promising to see them all in the morning. Alan gave up his room to Paul, who seemed to expect it, which left him to share the sitting room with Ches.

"I snore," Ches said. "You would be better off sharing with one of the others."

"I'm used to you," Alan said, yawning. "I'm exhausted. I probably won't even hear you." He yawned again.

"Very well."

The others said goodnight and trailed off to bed. Alan chose to sleep on the couch, while Ches curled up in a bed of soft blankets beside the fire.

"I have built up the fire, and this room will get very warm," Ches said.

Alan's only answer was to breathe heavily, his face flattened into a cushion, and his arm dangling off the side of the couch. He felt Ches watching him for a few moments, then came a soft footfall and the faint click of a door closing.

Alan opened his eyes and he sat up. His old suspicions of Ches had returned in full force, and he was determined to follow him. He got off the couch and slipped quietly out the front door.

Chapter Twenty-eight

QUEEN ROSE

H aspin hurried down the corridor. A smile hung upon his
lips. He had good news to relate for a change. She had
been extremely angry with him. Her ire at his failure to obtain
the magical flute had been terrible, but at least his plan with the
firebird had made up for it.

He entered the special chamber and waited. He did not have
to wait long.

"Ah, my friend, what news?" The voice was soft and cooed
gently, but Haspin knew how quickly it could change to fire and
ice.

He bowed deeply before the beautiful young woman who
stood tall before him.

"My queen," he said. "I am your humble servant."

"Are you my successful servant?"

"Yes, your majesty." Haspin straightened up but kept his eyes
lowered. "The firebird continues to produce gold, thanks to its
friendship with the prisoner."

"We are already two days behind schedule, thanks to your incompetence." There was an edge to her voice that could remove his skin, scale by scale. "Those feeble spells of yours will not keep the Diamonds in check long. Once free, they will surely track you down in these tunnels. How much gold?"

"We collect three times a day, and have more than sufficient for our needs."

"The chute?"

"Almost complete. The last two sections are being dealt with at this precise moment. As I say, we have more than enough gold for..."

"Keep collecting," Queen Rose said. "I like to be sure. Has work begun on the sphere?"

"Indeed it has. It should be complete before the night is through."

"It must be ready within three hours of darkness. I shall return then to commence proceedings. Arrange to get that girl up to my domain, she may be a useful bargaining tool."

Before Haspin could protest at the shortness of time, she had vanished, leaving only a trail of smoke.

"It shall be done, your majesty," he said. He had no choice.

Chapter Twenty-nine

THE GOLDEN CHUTE

Vicky brushed the fringe and sweat out of her eyes.
Applying gold leaf on walls and roof was gruelling work.
The narrow corridor had a low curved ceiling, which made
the job worse, for the heat was stifling and the air seemed
non-existent.

"Why do I have to do this? I'm not your slave." Resentment
bubbled inside Vicky. Bad enough being held prisoner without
being forced to work.

"You should not have broken your word," the guard said.
"You promised not to escape."

"Well, I didn't escape, did I?" Vicky grumbled. She hadn't
even tried. It was the Nuones who assumed it was an escape
attempt, when really she was searching for her telescope. She
couldn't let her captors know how important it was to her, in
case they looked at it more closely and discovered the flute. All
she had done was make a run for it to see if she could find the

Nuone who had taken her telescope. She hadn't got far before being caught.

Invisible cloaks make it too easy for them.

After that, she was assigned a different guard, and taken off fire-feeding duties.

"This way," the Nuone said grimly. He hadn't even given his name, making Otterbek seem friendly. He walked her back to what Vicky called the arrival chamber, the place where she had been caught and where she had been feeding the fire. She hadn't noticed the second exit from this cavern before, a narrow crevice in the rocky wall which led into a long rounded tunnel, rather like a chute, which ascended steeply in one direction, while the dip in the other direction seemed more gradual. Here she was handed a heavy pail full of liquid gold, and a large sponge-like brush and told to paint first the walls and then the ceiling. The floor was already golden-hued, and at regular intervals had what looked like lanterns in the floor, lighting up the chute.

Apart from having to bend and stretch, the gold was easy to apply. The worst part was that every time she needed to refill, she had to drag her bucket back to the first chamber.

"Why are you painting the place gold?" she said to her guard. "What's the point?"

"We cannot live without beauty," the Nuone said grimly.

After a day and a half of back-breaking labour, Vicky decided to forget her promise to what's-his-face and escape. In her eyes, a promise to the villain who captured her was no promise at all. She wasn't sure what Lucky would say about that.

Unfortunately, it was difficult to find another way out of the tunnels when she was watched so closely.

Vicky lost track of time, but she suspected the Nuones had her work at least double shifts. Anxious about Susan, who she hadn't seen for days, and terrified the flute's hiding place in her telescope had been discovered, she also ached all over. On top of all that she feared Lucky would never find them.

It was of small comfort that she had found her rhythm of slopping the gold onto the walls and ceilings. The liquid gold was still warm, wherever it came from. She also became adept at stretching it to cover more of the wall so she would have fewer return journeys. Each journey with the pail lengthened as she painted more of the tunnel.

"Hurry," her guard said at the start of her seventh shift in the tunnel. "Time is running out."

"For what?" Vicky had completed a large section and had almost reached the bend in the tunnel. "What's the rush?" Then, just to irk the guard, she added, "Where's my sister? When am I going home?"

"Shut up," the guard said.

Hours passed before she was allowed a break. The Nuone gave her some slightly brackish water and bread. It was better than nothing, and Vicky walked along the passageway, the ceiling almost touching her head, and tried to loosen her stiffening shoulders.

"Back to work now," the guard said after fifteen minutes.

"Don't you ever take a break?" Judging by the grim silence with which he met her question, he did not.

By her rough calculations she had been working all day. Her head ached, her neck and shoulders felt that they were on fire. At least the gold smelled sweetly, like rose petals.

The tunnel sloped downwards. Someone appeared around the corner, painting the walls ahead of her, moving towards her. A Nuone in a grey tunic and no cloak, who painted much faster than she could. He must have started at the far end.

She wished she knew where the tunnel was going. Perhaps it crossed back into Nivram. Maybe there was an exit among the Little Hills, a shorter way home. Unless it was going deeper into Paul's land. She had been underground five days (she thought) and she neither knew where Susan was, nor discovered what the Nuones were up to. Neither had she found a way out or how to get help. In fact, all she had done was aid the Nuones in their evil plan. It was a depressing thought. Oh, and lost both her telescope and Susan's flute.

I'm not leaving here without my gift or Susan's. She stood back as the other worker caught up with her and allowed him to complete the gap so that his last few brush strokes met up with hers.

"Good job." She nodded, and walked quickly past him, down the slope. She heard her guard call out.

"Just stretching my legs," she shouted back and broke into a run.

She rounded the corner and the golden tunnel levelled off. Panting, she ran for several minutes before the tunnel came to an abrupt end in a smooth gold circle. She pushed against it, in case it was a door, and searched for a hidden catch but found nothing. The tunnel ended in some kind of golden emblem.

It didn't make sense. Why excavate a tunnel that came to a dead end? Why sheath it completely with molten gold?

"Come back." Her guard finally caught up with her. He hadn't hurried, he must have known she was headed for a dead end.

The emblem on the door was a rose bud. Strange lettering encircled the image but Vicky could not read it. The rose held sufficient meaning, however, for a rose only meant one thing to Vicky.

Queen Rose.

She retraced her steps with the guard.

"I'm exhausted. Isn't there a short cut to my cell?"

The guard pointed a dagger at her. "Do not attempt to run like that again. You should know by now you cannot escape from here, but tomorrow you will be free."

Which meant that whatever their plan was, it would be put into action sometime between now and then. She'd like to stop it.

She yawned. "What time is it?"

The guard hesitated. "The moon is up." The Nuones did not reckon time as Vicky did.

Vicky yawned again. "Time for bed." She needed to see what lay at the other end of the tunnel, and retrieve her telescope. Her mind churned with plans, but the reality was as soon as she was back in her cell, she would be stuck. She needed to trick her guard in some way first, take his dagger and knock him out.

She accompanied him back up the tunnel, and picked up her bucket. The grey-clad Nuone had disappeared. It looked like their work was done, and the tunnel was completely coated with gold. As she followed the guard through the narrow passage, she decided she'd hit him with the heavy metal bucket as they entered the arrival chamber. He wouldn't expect it then.

As she braced herself to strike, the guard took a step into the arrival chamber and collapsed to the ground.

Somebody had got to him first.

Chapter Thirty

ALAN ENTERS THE TUNNELS

T he moon had risen, dappling the ground, making it easy for Alan to slip from shadow to shadow as he followed Ches.

Ches set out towards the Little Hills, as Alan expected. When Ches dismissed Paul's black bog as being of no interest, Alan felt certain it was the place. It amazed him that Lucky and Charlie hadn't picked up on it too. If only he could have discussed the matter with Cathy but he was on his own for this adventure.

The route to the peak of the Little Hills was steep and strewn with boulders. Ches's long stride easily covered the ground but Alan struggled to keep up. At least there was no danger of losing sight of him, for Ches made no attempt to conceal himself.

At the peak, Ches paused and looked back. Alan ducked behind a large boulder. Was it his imagination or had his quarry grown taller? Ches disappeared over the hill and Alan hurried after him.

The land over the border lay in deep shadow, with no sign of Ches. Alan pressed on, taking extra care as he started down the slope.

He didn't get far. An arm wrapped itself about his neck, choking him, and Ches hissed in his ear. "What are you doing, boy? Following me?"

Alan fought for air. The Nuone relaxed his grip a little and Alan was able to breathe.

"Well?"

Alan couldn't think of any excuse. "Yes," he gasped.

"Do it more quietly then." Ches released him, and Alan sat up, wheezing.

"Where are you going?" Alan whispered, once he had caught his breath.

"Where do you think?" Ches's claw covered Lucky's star, which faintly illuminated each of his three digits. The heat which Charlie's chip used to give was absent. Somehow that did not surprise Alan.

"You don't really need heat at night, do you?" he said.

Ches looked at him as if considering whether to reply or to squash him. To Alan's surprise, he spoke. "I'm used to it, and I like it, but the night air won't kill me that fast. Nuones believe it will kill them instantly, but it won't."

"You're not a Nuone, are you?" Alan didn't mean to blurt it out, because if Ches was pretending to be a Nuone, he would want to stop Alan from telling anyone else.

"No. Now get back to your bed and go to sleep, or else shut up and come with me."

Relieved that Ches wasn't going to kill him after all and no longer afraid of him, Alan scrambled to his feet, eager to find out what Ches was up to. "You're going to the black bog that Tremere mentioned, aren't you?"

"Yes, and I'd rather have you under my eye than fumbling after me, making enough noise to wake every Nuone in the place."

"I can be quiet."

"I heard you following me half an hour ago. Come on."

Ches had exceptional hearing, but Alan did not point that out. If Ches became irritated, he mightn't allow Alan accompany him into the Nuone camp. Alan wouldn't miss that for anything.

"Hold on to this and don't let go." Ches held out one end of a stick. "Whatever happens. These bog holes suck you in. You'll fall a thousand feet to your death unless you hang on to me."

It seemed an ordinary branch but Alan gripped the stick as tightly as he could with both hands. Ches moved forward, and without any warning disappeared into the ground, Alan fell in after him.

Abruptly his descent halted, he swung in the empty darkness, arms and shoulders aching, but he couldn't hold on. As his fingers slipped, a claw shot out of nowhere and grabbed him. Pressed against Ches's side, Alan caught an urgent whisper. "Don't move. Don't even breathe."

A tiny gleam of light showed momentarily before being extinguished. It was enough to show Ches clinging with one arm to the side of the pit, which fell away into darkness. Then Ches started to crawl.

It took a long time for Ches to reach the bottom. Alan didn't move, barely breathed in case he knocked Ches off the wall and sent them both tumbling to their deaths. Ches's arm was sure to tire and drop him, and this dread weighed upon Alan during the entire painful descent. It was a relief when Ches finally released him onto the floor of the pit. The darkness was so complete that Alan could hardly tell if his eyes were open or not.

"Are you all right, boy?" Ches's harsh whisper disturbed the silence.

Alan nodded, forgetting Ches could not see him.

Until Ches's Diamond badge glowed strongly.

"There you are." Ches sounded relieved. He raised the beam a little and pivoted on his feet to examine their surroundings.

A large circular area of soft black clay spread under their feet, and the walls of the pit rose into darkness. The floor of the pit was bare. Alan had expected it to be covered with bones but animals obviously had enough sense to keep away.

"We didn't save your life then, did we?" Alan blurted out the thought as it occurred to him. If the cold was not fatal to Ches, their ministrations in the dungeon in Thule had been a waste of time.

"This is no place to linger for a chat," Ches said. The light showed an exit from the pit and he moved towards it. "Yes, you probably did. I had been there a week in the damp and the cold, I was genuinely sick. Anea had left me there to rot."

Alan hastened after him. "Why didn't you escape?"

"I had nowhere to go, no way of getting out of Thule. And frankly, I do like the heat. Quietly now, this tunnel will lead us to the centre of things."

The roof of the tunnel was low, so Alan had to crouch to walk along it. Ches had been swallowed up by darkness, his eyesight as good as his hearing. Alan fumbled after him until he remembered that there were two Diamond chips, and his was the better one. He asked Sparkie to shed some light. "But dimly."

The chip obligingly glowed faintly, adequate to lighten the way and show Ches ahead, with shoulders hunched, who had managed to shrink enough to walk upright.

Ches stopped abruptly and Alan nearly bumped into him.

"How did you know?" Ches's harsh whisper reached him. "What did I do that gave me away? I've been successfully masquerading as a Nuone for years."

Alan tried to recall what had made him guess. "You're taller than the others. You know too much magic. I mean, you said Nuones only did simple tricks but then you seemed to know lots of magic. Also in the dungeon you said a few things that sounded more like...something else." He didn't want to say *Thulian*, because Thulians were bad, and Alan liked Ches, who had saved Cathy's life (twice), and probably his own.

Ches sighed. "Over-confident. I let my mask slip. Shouldn't have saved your sister, gave myself away there."

Alan grinned in the darkness. Ches's callous way of talking was clearly part of his act. Alan suspected Ches was in fact a big softy. Then Ches was gone again, darting around a sharp corner, so Alan ran to catch up.

Sometime later the tunnel ended in a well-lit cavern. Alan hadn't realised how chilly the passageway had been until he felt the warm air pushing in from the mouth of the tunnel.

Ches raised a claw to warn Alan to wait while he quietly exited the tunnel, but Alan kept behind him, almost stepping on his heels.

They walked out onto a ledge close to the cavern roof, overlooking a large chamber below where a huge fire roared, its smoke making Alan's eyes smart. Ches peered over a stone balustrade. After a moment he stepped back to Alan.

"Two guards below," he said quietly. "One is feeding the fire, the other is on watch duty. Stay here while I dispose of them."

"I'll help you." Alan said eagerly.

"*Stay!*"

Alan crept to the balustrade and looked down. A small figure shovelled fuel into the fire, stopping frequently to rub his forehead. He reminded Alan of the guards that stood at the base of the masters' platform in Thule, except this one wore a green cloak, untied and swept back over his shoulder. On the far side of the chamber, a large exit led into another tunnel, but there was no sign of a second guard.

Ches stood where the ledge met the cavern wall and placed his claw against the wall. A foot followed. Ches edged off the balcony and crept down the wall behind the Nuone feeding the fire, who seemed so intent on his work that he would never notice Ches.

But where was the second guard? Ches's eyes were sharper than Alan's but try as he might, Alan could glimpse no sign of a second guard. The chamber, other than the fire and its attendant, seemed totally empty.

Ches reached the ground, and took two steps forward before his arms shot out to grapple with the air. Then he lowered his invisible enemy to the floor and disappeared. At the same moment the body of a Nuone appeared on the ground. Seconds later, the Nuone at the fire dropped his shovel, struggled briefly before he too fell down.

Two minutes later Ches appeared on the balcony wearing a green cloak, like the one the fire tending guard had been wearing (which had mysteriously vanished as he fell to the ground). A second green cloak was draped over his arm, which he held out to Alan.

"What happened?" Alan asked. "How are there two guards now?"

"Cloaks of invisibility. Here, take it. Makes you difficult to see in these surroundings. Fortunately, the watch guard was facing the tunnel, not thinking anyone would approach this way. I didn't need it to deal with the other Nuone, but I wore it anyway."

Alan quickly fastened the cloak about his shoulders. A cloak of invisibility...how fantastic was that? He had gone from no magical gifts to two, and he didn't want to return either.

"See that golden button?" Ches pointed to the top button, the only one shaped as a dragon. "Press that once to disappear, and twice to reappear."

Alan pressed it once and looked down. He couldn't see his body any more. *Incredible.*

"It works better if you pull the hood over your head," Ches said.

His face must have been visible. Hastily Alan pulled up the hood so that it overshadowed his face. "Can you see me now?"

"I can, but nobody else will."

Alan pressed the dragon twice and he could see his feet once more, peering beneath the edge of the cloak.

"How can you see through the cloaks?"

"It's only side one magic, wouldn't fool anyone who knew side two or greater, but it will be useful for here. Most of these Nuones have not even got the base level."

Alan touched the soft shiny material, noticing that the cloak barely touched the floor, like Ches's one. "Can I keep it?"

Ches shrugged. "Not mine. Sylverine stole a whole load of these from Barne, he's pretty miffed with him. Are you done with questions now? I'll carry you down to the chamber and let us see if we can find our enemies."

Chapter Thirty-one

AN UNEXPECTED ENCOUNTER

"It's all right, Vicky, it's me." Alan's voice without Alan's body attached, coming directly after the mysterious collapse of her guard give Vicky such a fright that she cried out. It was even more startling when he appeared in front of her.

"How? What? Where?" Vicky stumbled over her questions.

Alan's face wore an enormous grin. "I've got an invisible cloak. See." He vanished and then re-appeared before her.

"I've seen them already on some of the guards around here," Vicky said, recovering. "But how did you get in here? Is Lucky with you?"

"No, but my friend Ches is. Ches? Will you show yourself to Vicky?"

"Reluctantly."

Vicky stepped back at the sight of Ches, but Alan said quickly. "He's good, he's with us."

"I'm with nobody other than myself," Ches corrected, his eyes darting watchfully around the room. "Save your explanations for later. What can you tell us about the set-up here?"

Vicky didn't know what to make of Ches, who looked like a stringier version of the Nuones she had met, but she was so happy to have help that she didn't worry about it. In as few words as she could manage, she told them about the golden chute, the emblem of Queen Rose, the dozens of guards, the other chamber where she met the two Nuones in charge and how they referred to their master, and how Susan had been taken away to another part of the underground tunnel.

"Whatever they are doing, they're doing it tonight," she finished with. "They said I'd be free tomorrow."

"Is that the tunnel?" Ches said, pointing to where Vicky's guard had fallen.

"Yes." Her guard was still breathing but she hoped he wouldn't wake up too soon. She stepped around him and slipped back into the passage.

"You say you've seen two large chambers?" Ches said. "The third one is the important one then."

"How do you know there's a third?" Vicky said.

"It's a basic pyramid shape. Nuones love triangles. I wonder what they have as the peak?" Ches said.

"Where's Lucky?" Vicky said in a low voice to Alan, in case Ches didn't know the Diamonds.

"She doesn't know we're here," Alan said airily. "Ches and I are doing our own investigation."

"What!" Vicky forgot she had done much the same thing.

"Ssh! And better make yourself disappear." Ches vanished as he spoke. "If we meet anyone, I will dispose of them."

"Don't go invisible," Vicky said quickly. "I'll feel like I'm talking to myself."

It was too late. Alan too had disappeared.

"Here it is," Vicky said, stepping into the chute. "I don't know what's at the top of it but if you go down, you'll find the panel with the rosebud." She felt someone push past her and guessed it was Ches judging by the deep inhaling.

"Allowing for slight deviations, this pathway is running due north-south, joining up some part of Paul's country to somewhere near that mountain of your Diamond friends," Ches said.

"Mount Slant?" Vicky said. If only she could break through that seal, maybe it opened right beside their cottage. On second thoughts, she hoped it didn't. She didn't want Nuones popping in and out of Nivram undetected.

"Or thereabouts. You say you travelled to one end of this?"

"Yes, left leads to the dead end."

"South," Ches said in a musing tone. "Let's see what is at the northern end."

"Wait," Vicky said. "What about Susan? She's locked up here somewhere. And my telescope was taken from me."

"I'm not making you come with us," Ches said. "I need to see what is at the far end. Afterwards we will look for your sister and your telescope."

"She could be at the other end of this tunnel," Alan said.

"Oh, all right." Vicky gave in. *"Please* show yourselves, or I won't know if I leave you behind or not."

With a shimmer both Alan and Ches appeared before her.

"Lead on then," Ches said.

It was very warm in the tunnel, and grew hotter the further she went. She walked as fast as she could, but as the slope grew steeper, her legs began to ache. Finally she stopped to catch her breath.

"We don't have much time," Ches said sourly, brushing past her.

Vicky caught Alan's eye.

"I forgot," Alan said. "You don't know. They attacked the Diamonds. Only for Ches, Lucky would be stuck inside the Rock. And Cathy would be dead."

Vicky's mouth dropped open. "What?"

"Tell you later," Alan said, continuing up the slope.

"Tell me now," Vicky said, running after him. She hadn't considered what might be happening back in Nivram, other than assuming everyone would be frantically searching for her and Susan. What she thought had been a plot to steal the flute now looked like something much bigger.

Ches stopped a few paces short of a large, round, door-less gap that opened into a chamber. The third chamber.

"Alan," Ches said. "Hide yourself." He disappeared as he spoke. "This way we can investigate without being seen."

"What will I do?" Vicky said.

"Wait for us."

Vicky sighed. She hoped Ches would be quick for sooner or later the unconscious guard would be found and the Nuones were sure to find her.

Chapter Thirty-two

THE THIRD CHAMBER

Ches pushed Alan ahead into the chamber.

"If Sylverine is there, he will see me immediately," Ches hissed.

This chamber reminded Alan of the first one, with its high domed ceiling and triangular hearth with a blazing fire. In the heart of this fire a huge sphere blazed gold and red. Two Nuone guards stood on a metal platform by the fire. One fed the flames with armfuls of gleaming feathers while the second, using a long-handled implement, poured a golden syrup over the sphere.

Thick, dark smoke wafted from the fire, spicy and pungent, tickling Alan's throat. He hurried past it to look at a shiny black throne on the far side. Beyond the throne were double doors made of gold. A black rug with a red rose woven in its centre was placed before the throne, one more sign that Queen Rose was behind the attack.

Alan didn't think either of the Nuone guards could be Sylverine. He waited for Ches to nudge him onwards, but at that moment the doors burst open. A Nuone, wearing a cloak of gold with a large golden pin and carrying a small black box, entered. He placed the box carefully before the throne, peering sharply about the room.

Alan shrank into the shadows, fearful he had accidentally pressed the dragon twice and this newcomer could see him.

A thundering of steps sounded in the golden tunnel and a dozen Nuone guards entered. Vicky was in the middle of them, several daggers held to her throat.

"What have we here?"

"A spy, found in the tunnel, Lord Haspin," one of the guards said.

Haspin stepped in front of Vicky. "It's the troublesome prisoner. We should have handed her over to the queen with the other one. What were you doing in the chute?"

"I was admiring the work I did earlier," Vicky said, trying to shake her arm free from the soldier who gripped it.

Alan's awe at Vicky's quick thinking turned to shock as Haspin struck her. Vicky staggered back, blood trickling down her chin.

"We'll deal with you later." Haspin turned away and stepped towards Alan. "Our queen is due."

Before Alan could react, a claw shot out and grabbed his shoulder, ripping away the cloak in one swift movement. Yellow eyes glared viciously at him. Alan tried to push him off but Haspin's grip was too firm.

Haspin shook Alan hard. "What are you doing here? Where did you get that cloak? Answer me!" He shook Alan again.

"Back there," Alan gasped, shocked his cloak lay in green shreds on the floor. Where was Ches?

"Lord Haspin!" One of the guards spoke urgently.

Haspin glanced towards the throne, released Alan, and said, "Keep a close watch on him."

Another guard seized Alan and bundled him next to Vicky.

Thick oily smoke poured out of the black box on the rug, growing denser as it coiled slowly into the air. A woman's form took shape, then solidified; it seemed she was truly there. Tall and beautiful, with flowing black curls and cruel red lips set in a deadly pale face.

Beside him, Vicky gasped. "Can't be her!"

Alan had never seen the woman before but knew at once who she was.

Queen Rose.

She looked at the glowing sphere and her lips curved into a smile. "It looks good, Haspin."

Haspin bowed low. "To please you is our greatest honour."

"But how will you launch it? Where is your...catapult?"

"It will be here any moment, Queen."

As he spoke the door opened once more. Two solemn looking Nuones entered and held both doors fully open. The sound of scuffling came from the corridor, and the air grew even hotter.

More Nuones entered. These pulled on long golden chains, dragging something behind them. Alan wondered what weapon they were hauling in, and gasped when he saw the creature squeezed through the door. It had to be Ches's firebird.

Queen Rose's plan was no clearer to him, except it involved the firebird, the golden sphere, and the tunnel.

The firebird's wings pressed tightly against its sides, and its head hung low. Through the golden feathers that clung to its body Alan saw smooth golden skin. Its blue eyes held a mixture of sorrow and dread. When its gaze alighted upon Queen Rose, it trembled with fear and cowered still further.

"There, there, my pretty," the witch said in an insincere cooing voice. "You're here to help us."

The firebird tried to back away as far as possible from her, but the chains that held it prevented it from moving far.

"Tie down the creature," Haspin ordered.

Alan hadn't noticed the strong metal rings in the floor. The four chains that bound the firebird were attached firmly to these rings, and the Nuones who had been holding the firebird looked relieved. The firebird was now fixed directly in front of the fire, which lay between it and the golden tunnel.

"You may stop that now," Haspin said to the Nuone pouring the golden liquid over the sphere.

The Nuone replaced the ladle in the pot, bowed slightly and stepped away. The Nuone feeding the fire continued to do so.

"Fire fed on golden feathers, a sphere constructed from them and sealed by their oil," Queen Rose said. "Perfect."

With the cessation of the liquid being poured onto the sphere, the smoke that came from the fire diminished and shrank away. In its absence Queen Rose's eyes fell upon Alan and Vicky.

Her voice sharpened, some of the pleasure driven from her face. "What have we here?"

"Two prisoners," Haspin said smoothly. "Which I shall deal with immediately after the launch."

Queen Rose glared at Vicky.

"One of these I know. You should have sent them to me earlier. That one is trouble." Her eyes dwelled on Alan for a few uncomfortable minutes. "He's another of them. Maybe this can be turned to my advantage. Three prisoners are better than one. A bargaining tool, if there is anything left to bargain with." She laughed.

Alan was not going to be used as some kind of hostage by Queen Rose. All he needed was a plan. He had come up with one to escape the Nuone prison. Surely he could come up with something now.

"There will be nothing left afterwards," Haspin said, sending a chill rippling through Alan. Lucky was right, Queen Rose was scheming to destroy the Diamonds.

"Bring these two miserable creatures to my domain afterwards, along with your companions," the witch said. "Let us get this fireball upon its way."

"It won't work," Vicky said, her voice trembling slightly.

Queen Rose's eyes darted towards her. "What won't?"

"Ignore her, my queen," Haspin said urgently. "Let us start."

"You are right, my slave."

"Your plan won't work," Vicky spoke louder. "It's doomed. The Diamonds know all about it."

Alan wished they did.

Hatred spread all over the witch's face. "They can't, they can't."

"Why do you think my brother is here?" Vicky nodded at Alan. "He arrived only moments ago to distract your soldiers while the Diamonds are destroying your work."

"Really?" Queen Rose seemed calmer now. "Well, boy, what exactly is my scheme? Tell me what you know, and I may let you go."

Alan licked his lips. He wished Vicky had told him her plan. He didn't know what she expected him to say, but he did his best.

"You want to turn Crocodile Lake to gold." He remembered Ches's words. "This will kill the guardians and end the Diamond realm. But they know all about it and are ready for you."

There was an arrested look in the witch's eyes.

"Wrong," she said. "Yet not so far from the truth. Haspin, how do they know so much?"

"Lucky guess, Queen," Haspin said sourly. "But let us delay no further."

Queen Rose nodded. "Proceed."

"What is your plan?" Vicky said.

"I shall not ruin the surprise," the witch said, smirking.

The ball, the chute... It began to make sense to Alan.

"You're going to send this sphere down the chute...into Crocodile Lake?" The words burst out although he meant to stay quiet.

Queen Rose looked pleased.

"Yes, imagine this wonderful fireball rushing through the chute of gold, pounding into Crocodile Lake, and leaving a great big hole. Imagine that! What an impact! The fireball shooting through the waters of the lake, causing havoc before it finally fizzles out... By then there will be no lake left. The water will pour out the hole, through the tunnel, and burst through this very chamber at the speed of light."

"Come, Queen," Haspin reminded her.

"Yes. Alas we need our friend here to launch it. It can neither be built not launched by hand but formed only from this creature's gold and started by its breath. Creature, when I give you the word, you shall give a great big breath and blow so hard that the sphere flies down the tunnel."

The firebird looked in terror at the witch.

Alan couldn't tell if the firebird would do the witch's bidding or not. His brain turned sluggish, unable to think of any way to stop her.

"She'll trick you," Vicky shouted at Haspin. "You'll be left with us to die here."

Alan didn't think Vicky's attempt to cause trouble would work but Haspin had a touch of concern in his eyes when he addressed the witch. "The connection is in place, is it not? Your castle awaits us?"

"The moment you hear the impact of sphere against lake, direct all your men to leave."

Haspin nodded to two of his guards who immediately started to swarm up the rope to the small balcony above.

"You do not trust me, Haspin." The witch's mocking voice filled the chamber. "When I have trusted you."

"Like you, I intend to err on the side of caution," Haspin said. Alan was surprised to see that he had dropped some of his earlier obsequiousness.

Queen Rose turned to Alan and Vicky.

"You shall leave with Haspin before the waters flood this chamber and erupt over...what was that little fool's name? Oh yes, Prince Paul's land. I am not sure how much of his country will remain permanently under water, for who knows the depths of Crocodile Lake, but it should cause him problems."

"So it's the Kingdom of Kyle you want to destroy, not the Diamonds?" Alan shouted at the witch. Paul had played an important role in defeating the witch the last time, he knew. "For some kind of stupid revenge!"

Vicky had also played her part, Alan remembered, and felt even sicker, for it meant Queen Rose probably had something terrible in mind for his sister.

"The guardians *will* wake, the Diamonds' tenure over these lands *will* end, and I don't expect to be troubled by them anymore. Washing away the Kingdom of Kyle is a bonus." Queen Rose glanced up towards the balcony. "Your friends are back, Haspin."

The two Nuones signalled to Haspin, and he nodded in acknowledgement.

"I apologise for doubting you, my queen." Hapsin bowed deeply as he spoke.

"All is forgiven," the witch said sweetly. Haspin looked a little unsettled by these words.

"Firebird, set the sphere upon its path," Queen Rose commanded.

The firebird looked mutinous, kept its mouth firmly closed, and crouched close to the ground.

"You do not want to anger me," the witch said in steely tones. The firebird did not budge. "I have a friend of yours here with me in my realm. Someone you should be pleased to see."

She reached out an arm and Susan appeared before them, as if the witch were dragging her by the hair yet not touching her. Susan was weeping in pain.

The firebird looked up, rose slightly and made an alarmed sound.

"Yes, your little friend here might get hurt if that sphere isn't launched."

Susan's eyes were on Queen Rose as if that was all she saw, but at these words she looked blankly over Alan's head.

"Don't listen to her, whoever you are, don't listen to her," she said desperately.

Susan's head jerked to one side, as if she were a puppet on a string. She screamed but the witch moved her arm, as if to toss her aside, and Susan vanished.

Alan struggled to free himself of the guards, but his arms were held too tightly.

He remembered Charlie's chip in his pocket. If only he could seize it and blast the witch with all of Charlie's power! But he could not reach into his pocket where Sparkie lay.

Beside him, Vicky shouted at Queen Rose.

"She's got Susan! Let her go, you ugly witch."

The witch paid no attention. She leaned towards the firebird, her eyes burning.

"Launch, firebird, launch the sphere!"

"Wait." Ches stepped out of the golden chute. His cloak was open and thrown back, and as Alan watched, he grew taller, his ragged tunic turned to gold and silver, while his face narrowed and his eyes grew smaller. "Wait. I am Zeroxian the Thulian, and I am here to stop you, Abcadarniz."

Chapter Thirty-three

THE SPHERE

A surge of relief ran through Alan at Ches's words. Ches would stop Queen Rose.

The witch merely laughed.

"Oh, I have come on a long way since my days in Thule. Even then you were no match for me, Zeroxian."

"You destroyed our kind, Abcadarniz. I cannot forget that. I will not allow you destroy others."

The witch turned to the firebird. "Launch the sphere. Or see your friend die."

The firebird rose to its feet and pulled at its shackles, but they held firm. Ches produced a long sword and hacked at one of the chains.

"Launch the sphere," the witch shrieked. "Haspin, stop him."

Half a dozen Nuones ran over to Ches, but at a glance from him, they fell back. Servants of the Thulians still. They looked in confusion to their leader.

Haspin cast aside his cloak and grew rapidly to the same height as Ches. His bronze garments shone.

"I too am Thulian," he announced, "Though perhaps you do not recognise me, Ches."

Chas paused in his attack on the chains and glanced over. "You, Haspin? I knew another hid among the Nuones, but I thought Sylverine."

Haspin laughed shortly and produced a sword that gleamed more wickedly than Ches's.

"Sylverine! A good Nuone, one of the best, but only a Nuone!"

Ches resumed hacking at the chains when Haspin rushed at him.

"Launch the sphere," the witch chanted. "Launch it, beast."

The chain flew free and hit one of the guards holding Alan, who staggered back. Ches turned in time to parry Haspin's blow and then they fell upon each other, swords ringing out, and sparks flying. The Nuone guards pulled daggers from their belts, ready to assist Haspin.

"Launch the sphere," Queen Rose screamed.

"Attack this enemy," Haspin shouted. The Nuones ran to his aid.

The firebird pulled and strained at the other chains.

Alan snatched Sparkie from his pocket. "Stop them, Sparkie! Help Ches!"

He couldn't think of the rhyme, but it didn't seem to matter. Light blazed from the chip as Alan turned it towards the Nuone guards. The first one screamed, dropped his weapon and threw his hands to his eyes.

"Quick, another," Vicky said, pointing.

Alan quickly directed Sparkie to one about to stab Ches in the back. As the guard collapsed, his knife slashed Ches in the leg instead. Ches staggered but regained his balance. Sparks ran up and down the swords of the Thulians, and began to lick at the blades. Vicky called Alan's attention again. He swept around in a circle, blinding as many of the guards as he could, but it proved only a temporary measure. After a few moments they recovered their sight and jumped to their feet once more.

Ches leaped onto the black throne, and, lunging forward, the point of his blade pierced Haspin in the shoulder. Haspin cried out but rallied, and as he did, the throne burst into flames. Ches continued to fight for a moment before jumping off, his tunic singed. Both blades were now on fire, causing the guards to stay well clear.

Snap! Another chain broke free, flying across the room and knocking over the pot of liquid that had been used to coat the sphere. Steam rose as it made contact with the ground, the guards screamed and ran away from its outspread fingers.

"Launch the sphere or she dies," Queen Rose screamed.

Snap! The third chain broke, catching Ches around the legs and bringing him crashing to the floor. Haspin pounced, stood on his chest, and held his sword directly over Ches's head.

"Death to my enemies," he cried, but as he was about to plunge the flaming sword into Ches's heart, Alan sent a flash of light straight into Haspin's eyes. Blinded temporarily, he hesitated. At the same moment the firebird broke free of the final chain, stretched its body, half-expanded its wings and opened its jaw in an agonising cry of pain. Flames shot out and engulfed Haspin, Ches, and every nearby Nuone.

The firebird roared again, and the great ball of flaming liquid gold swayed in the fire, then tipped over and rolled across the floor and disappeared with a rush into the golden tunnel.

Chapter Thirty-four

ESCAPE FROM THE TUNNELS

A fter that everything seemed to happen in slow motion to
Vicky.

Queen Rose crowed triumphantly and vanished.

The firebird beat its wings and rose towards the roof.

Haspin, receiving the full blast of the flames, staggered about
the cavern on fire from head to foot before collapsing to the
ground.

Three or four Nuones rolled across the floor to extinguish the
blaze, while the rest of the guards raced for the rope and began
to frantically climb to the balcony.

It dawned on Vicky that the witch's plan had worked, the
fiery sphere had set off on its journey to Crocodile Lake. How
long before the tunnels were flooded?

Familiar voices reached her and she saw Yvonne at the tunnel
entrance, Lucky blazing from her shoulder.

"Alan and Ches first," she heard Lucky's clear silvery voice say.

Then Yvonne hugged her and asked her something but Vicky looked for Alan and his friend. Ches lay on the ground, clothes and skin badly charred. Alan knelt beside him, calling his name.

Lucky alighted on Ches's shoulder. "He's still alive but barely."

"Can you cure him, Lucky?" Alan said.

"Normally, yes, but I'm still very weak," Lucky said.

Alan hadn't been touched by the fire but the reek of burned flesh was rampant. Vicky saw Haspin's blackened body and shuddered.

"We have to hurry," Vicky said, looking away. "The sphere is going to blow a hole in Crocodile Lake and this place will be flooded in a couple of minutes."

"Don't worry," Lucky said. "I sent some Diamonds to stop it. We've been hiding in the wings for a while. I tried to stop Ches from coming out to fight, but that was impossible." A spark flew out of Lucky as she spoke but fizzled away before reaching Ches. "Allow me a few more minutes to collect my strength."

"Susan's in the witch's castle," Vicky said urgently. "We've got to get her while she's still close. We can follow those Nuones escaping to join the witch. We can't wait any longer."

"We've another problem." Yvonne pointed upwards.

Above their heads, the firebird pounded the ceiling. Fragments of earth fell away and crashed to the floor near them.

At the same moment light poured into the chamber from the tunnel, as hundreds of Diamonds streamed in. They flowed up to Lucky.

"We couldn't stop it, Princess," they cried. "Only turn it back. It's on its way now."

"We must leave immediately," Lucky said. "Follow the firebird."

"What about Ches?" Alan said.

"Carry Ches," Lucky told the Diamonds, and Ches was instantly borne upwards, as if on a carpet of stars rising to the roof. "Take the children too, they won't be able to climb out in time."

A moment later, Alan and Yvonne floated upwards, Alan looking nervous but excited, and Yvonne's eyes shut in terror.

A huge piece of ceiling fell to the floor, partly covering Haspin's body.

"The gifts!" Vicky broke away from the Diamonds. She was not going to leave without her telescope.

Hot air blasted from the golden tunnel, she could hear the rumble of the sphere approaching, and the concerned song of the Diamonds. Rocks and earth rained down as she leaped over the debris and crouched by Haspin.

She felt no pity for him, only relief that his face was hidden.

It must be here, she thought, and, though her stomach churned, she quickly pulled at his clothes.

Her telescope hung in its velvet pouch around his neck, completely undamaged. She grabbed it and it broke free of Haspin, as if of its own accord, at the moment she was lifted into the air.

The rest of the cavern roof collapsed as the firebird broke through and swooped upwards. The Diamonds followed, blazing with light, pushing aside the falling debris. Vicky was lifted past several Nuones scrambling up a rope to the gallery, then she left them behind as she was carried upwards, through the broken ceiling, and up through the pit towards the surface.

She looped the pouch about her neck and pressed it close to her heart.

Looking back, she could see the huge fire that had once housed the sphere decreasing in size.

The next moment the sphere hurtled itself into the fire, and a gust of hot air shot up through the pit, rocking Vicky and the Diamonds. Her eyes watered with sudden tears, and she heard the cry of a Nuone as it lost its hold on the rope and fell to the floor below.

The sphere's liquid gold had seeped away, and its heart now burned a fiery red. It was going to explode, and she silently urged the Diamonds to hurry.

Which they did.

A few seconds later the cool night air brushed her cheeks under the velvet sky covering the ceiling of the world. She tried to figure out where she was. Somewhere in the Little Hills, she guessed. The Diamonds set her gently on the ground, and she noticed with wonder that her clothes were scorched in places.

"Run," Alan shouted, from some way off. "Lucky said to run."

Vicky raced after Alan and Yvonne who had ducked behind large boulders.

The force of the explosion took her by surprise. The ground shook, debris flew up in the air and rained about her, and she was flung off her feet and thrown across the ground.

Everything hurt. She lay still until the earth stopped shaking and she heard Yvonne call her name.

"I'm fine," she said weakly.

She thought of Susan and managed to roll onto her back, expecting to see Queen Rose's castle floating above their heads, perhaps with a rope ladder hanging down for the Nuones to charge up.

It looked Queen Rose had lied to Haspin, for there was no sign of her castle waiting to collect fleeing Nuones. Queen Rose had abandoned them to their fate.

Stars crowded the sky, except for one large dark patch moving rapidly away, no longer directly over the flame-licked pit but heading south towards Nivram and Crocodile Lake. The witch probably wanted to observe the lake rapidly empty its waters.

"Lucky, she's getting away," Vicky shouted. "Susan!" It was pointless to call her sister's name, but she did anyway.

"She's moving fast," Lucky said, sounding surprisingly near.

Vicky pushed herself upright. Yvonne and Lucky were right behind her.

"We have to go after her! What about Charlie?" Vicky remembered the last time when Charlie had raced against the witch. "Where is he?"

"He's with Tremere and Paul, guarding the other pit, the one we came in by."

So Queen Rose was going to escape, and take Susan with her! Why wasn't Lucky doing something to stop her? Vicky clenched her fists in fear for her sister's life.

"What's that?" Yvonne said, pointing above her head.

Vicky gazed upwards.

Flying high and swooping as if delighted to be free, the firebird glowed like a warm flame, tracing circles of light in the sky.

All of a sudden, it dived and darted after the black outline of Queen Rose's castle.

Chapter Thirty-five

REUNITED

Queen Rose's castle sped south, towards Mount Slant. Without thinking, Vicky started after it, knowing she would never catch up. Yvonne was right beside her. Gasping, panting, Vicky sprinted, her knees and palms grazed painfully from her fall, while the Diamonds cascaded over the ground like a torrent of white foam.

Clutching her side to ease the pain, Vicky scrambled down towards the moonlit waters of Crocodile Lake, smooth and undisturbed by the explosion of the golden sphere. The witch's castle veered, as if she had become aware of the firebird following like a golden arrow. The dark patch obscuring the stars moved faster and farther away but the firebird increased its speed even more. Moments later it disappeared into the darkness of the castle.

Vicky strained her eyes to make out what was happening. Would the firebird appear again? Or had Queen Rose claimed yet another victory?

The sky lightened, a brightness coming from the west. Vicky inhaled sharply. The edges of the cloud had turned golden.

The firebird had set the flying castle alight.

Yvonne caught up and panted beside her.

"I didn't think it could burn," Vicky whispered, meaning the strange black metal the pyramid was made of.

"The firebird is a creature of Thule, and a powerful one too. As is Witch Rose," Lucky said from Yvonne's shoulder.

"What about Susan?" Vicky bit her lip. If the castle burned...

"There's nothing I can do," Lucky said.

In silence they stood and watched while the grounds of Queen Rose's domain, the cloud, glowed brightly and fell to ash.

Soon Vicky could make out the shape of the pyramid castle and witness how strongly it blazed. The firebird was now visible, swooping and gliding in delight while its enemy burned. Vicky could only think of Susan, with not even her flute to comfort her. She blinked back tears.

A distant bang shattered the silence and half the pyramid broke into pieces, like a million stars shooting in different directions.

Another explosion and the rest of the witch's home fell apart and scattered across the sky. The firebird still swooped and turned circles in total abandonment, while great burning pieces of pyramid fell to earth.

Vicky swallowed hard, dropped to the ground and buried her head in her arms. Yvonne sat beside her, put an arm about her shoulders and hugged her until the flotsam drifting in the sky burned out.

"We better find Alan and the others," Lucky said.

Vicky wiped the unshed tears from her eyes, nodded briefly and got up.

"Does that mean we are free of Queen Rose forever?" Vicky said but what she really meant was if it were possible that Susan could somehow still be alive. "Nothing could have survived that explosion."

"Looks like it," Lucky said quietly. "Are you sure Susan was in the castle?"

"I suppose not," Vicky said. "I know the witch made it look that way. But if she wasn't in the castle, then we left her behind in the tunnels."

She could see the circle in the ground ahead, the exit of the pit above the third chamber, which glowed brightly in the night. What chance had Susan of surviving that?

"We do not yet know how far those tunnels extend or how much damage was done underground. Don't assume that all hope is lost," Lucky said.

Despite Lucky's words, Vicky didn't feel any better and she struggled to retrace her steps. She clutched her pouch, hoping her magical gift would help her bear the pain.

Alan waited for them beside Ches's prone body.

"Ches is really sick," Alan said urgently. "He's badly burned. Lucky, can you cure him?"

Lucky shone a little brighter. "I will do my best."

Alan looked relieved. "So is the witch finally dead?" he said. He mustn't have realised that Susan had been in the castle, and Vicky did not want to tell him. Not yet, not until they were sure.

"Yes," Vicky said. "What will we do now, Lucky?"

"We must get Ches back to the Rock. If he survives the journey, I have every expectation that we shall cure him." Lucky sounded confident.

"Couldn't you do it here?" Alan said.

"I am too weak, Alan. Best chance is if we get him close to home."

Alan's face fell but before he could react, a hoarse voice croaked his name.

"Alan."

Vicky, who thought Ches as good as dead, jumped at the sound of his voice.

"Alan, I'm afraid I shall not survive," Ches whispered. "I want to give you this." His hand rose up but then dropped down. Gripped between two fingers was some shimmering green material, part of the cloak secreted within Ches's tunic.

"Hang on to it, you'll need it yourself," Alan said, grinning.

"Looks like Ches may not need my help to recover," Lucky said. "I see Paul and Tremere coming this way. They must have seen the explosion."

Vicky cleared her throat. Beside her, Yvonne was silently crying. "What about Susan? Where shall we start the search for her?"

"How about over there?" Alan pointed behind her.

Vicky swung around. The firebird was flying low in the sky now, not far away. In a better mood she would have appreciated the graceful way it flew, the beauty of its fiery golden body and long delicate wings, so well defined against the night. But now all she could think was of the small dark figure that clung to its back.

The firebird flew closer, and finally landed by the glowing pit.

Susan slipped off the firebird's back, ready to greet the others when they ran over.

"Susan, we thought you were dead!" Yvonne sobbed.

"No, I'm fine," Susan said, though she looked pale and shocked. "Takes a little while to get used to flying like that."

"Did the firebird catch you mid-air?" Vicky said, talking quickly to hide her overwhelming relief. "As you fell from the sky?"

"No." Susan put a hand on the firebird's side and rubbed it tenderly. "I was in the witch's throne room. She had me immobilised in some way. I could move my head, but that was all. The firebird set the gardens on fire first, I think, before breaking into the throne room. I don't think the witch was very happy about seeing her beloved statues go up in smoke. She battled with my friend, but the firebird chased her away, picked me up, and off we went, getting out in time before the flames ripped the castle apart."

"I thought the king turned her into a lizard," Alan said. "But she looked a full-size witch to me."

"She projected that image," Susan said. "She is like a small lizard, but still terrifying." She shivered as she spoke.

"Thank you," Lucky said to the firebird. "We are in your debt."

The firebird lowered its head to the ground, as if bowing to the Diamond.

"You'll always be my friend," Susan said, rubbing its forehead. "I know you want your freedom but perhaps you'll come and visit."

The firebird sounded like it was purring.

Chapter Thirty-six

EXPLANATIONS

"And to think I missed all the fun," Cathy said, disgusted.

The morning was overcast, and Ches took one look at the sky and hurriedly pressed the star Lucky had given him to generate some warmth.

"Shocking," he said.

"At least you nearly died twice," Alan said. "And had all the excitement of being caught in a monstrous beast's mouth."

Cathy instinctively touched her side. It was tender still, although she was much better after a good night's sleep. She was sorry to learn that the rest of her family had been out battling Queen Rose without her. She had never seen the evil witch and was quite envious of Alan. It looked like she would never get the chance now.

Yvonne shuddered. "Don't talk of such horrors, Alan. I know I should be used to the two of you getting into trouble, but somehow I don't think I ever will."

Cathy didn't bother pointing out that Yvonne was just as good as getting into trouble as she and Alan were. They sat by the shores of Crocodile Lake, the waters serene and impenetrable as ever. The Nilkens had spread out rugs and cushions for the children to relax upon while they waited for the arrival of Lucky, Charlie, and the king. The Nilkens had, as always, provided a delicious repast, a late breakfast or early lunch for those who had only gone to bed as the moon had set.

The firebird was there too. It sat quietly beside Susan, its head in her lap. Cathy could feel its body heat from where she sat and was glad of it. She longed to make friends with the firebird but so far the firebird made it clear it only wanted to be with Susan. That didn't stop Cathy smiling at it and softly saying hello.

Vicky gave a great yawn. "I'm exhausted. Six hours sleep is just not sufficient. Oh Susan, I forgot to give this back to you." To Cathy's astonishment, Vicky unscrewed the top of the telescope, and emptied out Susan's flute.

"I knew you'd keep it safe." Susan slipped the flute back into its own pouch slung about her neck.

"Here's Lucky," Cathy said. She leaned over Tremere, lying on his back asleep, and shook his shoulder. "Wake up."

The King of the Diamonds was perched on a small throne, his usual sparkle extinguished. After greeting everyone, he sat quietly, listening but not talking.

"I'm sure everyone has a lot of questions," Lucky said. "But I think Ches should speak first."

"Me?" Ches had a wary look in his eye.

"Yes. You need to fill us in on the Thulian you struggled with last night, why he is involved, who is Sylverine, why you pretended to be a Nuone, and so on."

"I do?" Ches scratched his ear. "Oh, very well. I am certain you Diamonds know of our troubles, but for the sake of our young friends here I shall tell a brief version of the tale.

"Thule is the guardian of one quarter of this globe, as you no doubt are aware. He left a wonderful species in charge of much of his land, the place you call Thule, though we do not know it by that name, as well as many other lands, while he went off on his own business. I do not believe he took his responsibilities too seriously, but that's another story."

"Keep to the point," the king roused himself to say in a weak voice.

Ches looked a little disgruntled by the interruption. "To get to the essence of the story, we were left to our own devices..."

Cathy's mind drifted off as Ches explained the triangular magic and told the story of Thule giving the country to the Nuones.

"So you think Haspin betrayed the location of the Goldener city to Witch Rose, and after she had it destroyed, he crept back to your city?" Lucky's words brought Cathy back to the conversation.

"Yes, and disguised himself as a Nuone. As I had done earlier. Neither of us saw through the other's disguise." Ches coughed, cleared his throat, and took a drink of some strange smelling liquid that the Nilkens had made up on his instructions. "I assumed Haspin the Thulian had perished with the rest of the

Goldener people. Instead, Haspin the traitor lived on among us, waiting upon his call from his queen."

"What about Slith... Sylverine?" Paul said. "Isn't he the main one here?"

Ches took another drink. "Sylverine is a Nuone. He once served Abcadarniz. He may even have helped Haspin hide when he returned."

"You thought Sylverine stole the firebird?" Cathy said, remembering what Ches had said in the prison.

"I still do. He and thirty other Nuones disappeared the same time as the firebird, it did not take a genius to know who was behind it. Then my two friends here turned up with stories of an attack upon the Diamonds. I was curious and travelled with them. And once you mentioned Abcadarniz, I knew the time had come to avenge my people."

"Will the people of Thule never learn to keep away from that which is forbidden?" the king spoke irritably.

"Curiosity and a thirst for power are forever in our natures," Ches said.

"You recognised the black bog I mentioned as a sign that Sylverine was there, didn't you?" Tremere said.

"I had heard of its use. My instinct is never wrong."

"Why did you all turn up last night?" Alan said. "I thought I was the only one on to Ches."

Ches bowed in Lucky's direction. "Not the only one, I believe."

"I owe you an apology, Ches," Lucky said. "I was suspicious, so I added a little extra spell of my own to the star I gave you."

"I suspected as much," Ches said, though from his airy manner, Cathy wondered if he was covering up the fact he hadn't guessed at all. "I was happy to get there first."

Cathy shivered. Queen Rose had so nearly exacted revenge, and a lot of Nuones had died. "I'm glad she's gone." Lucky glowed strangely so Cathy quickly added: "She *is* gone, isn't she?"

"The Nilkens have been collecting the debris from the pyramid all morning," Lucky said. "Much less than expected. The flame from the firebird must have obliterated most of it. No sign of any body either. Don't worry. She is banned from setting foot on our soil, so even if she survived the fire, the explosion, and the fall, she could not land here."

"What if she did?" Vicky said.

"Father?" Lucky looked to the king.

"She would not dare defy me," the king said.

"Self-destruct," Lucky said, fortunately able to interpret his answer.

If Cathy was fully recovered, she would have whooped at the news that Queen Rose could never bother them again. Despite never seeing the witch, she had the greatest fear of her, Queen Rose even haunting her dreams since she was ill.

"I know the firebird's feathers turned golden after we became friends," Susan said sadly. "I didn't mean to help Haspin, but I'm not sorry. The firebird needed a friend."

"I helped too," Vicky said gloomily. "I gave them your flute and my telescope so we couldn't escape, and then I painted the golden tunnel for them."

Cathy looked at her sisters, aghast. Lucky sparkled a little. "Don't be too hard on yourselves. You had no choice. If you hadn't befriended the firebird, Susan, Witch Rose would have got away with it. If you hadn't hidden the flute, Vicky, Witch Rose could have used it instead of the feathers days earlier."

Charlie spoke for the first time. He had been very quiet up to this point, and Cathy was worried about him. "Her magic would not be powerful enough on its own to destroy Crocodile Lake. She needed the firebird's power; the flute was probably an attempt at a backup plan."

A light breeze blew off the lake and Cathy shivered a little. She hoped it was the last they would see of Queen Rose.

"Seems like you are done with me." Ches stood and stretched. "Perhaps the firebird would give me a lift home. Fang deserves to be destroyed but once the firebird returns to the city, Fang will slink back to the desert."

"You are welcome to stay here, Ches," Lucky said. "Where you don't have to live in hiding."

"Thank you, but I do miss the sun. And I hear you have something called... rain? Not for me, I thank you."

"You should go back in your true form," Lucky said. "I am sure Thule would understand, and think what respect you would get from the Nuones."

"The last of the Thulians," Ches mused. "No, I'd only be tempted like the rest. Let me live among the Nuones, unnoticed and undisturbed."

"I doubt if you will be unnoticed, Ches," Lucky said with a smile.

"Excuse me." Susan's voice shook a little. "There is something you should know. The firebird is not going back."

"Not going back!" Ches roared. "It has to! Thule placed it there. It has no choice. It must guard and protect us. How else will the rivers run with gold?"

"She's not going back," Susan said, her hands trembling. "She hates it there. The snake terrifies her. She's miserable."

Sympathy for the firebird flooded through Cathy. The firebird was right. Fang was terrifying and the firebird should never go back. It was cruel to expect it to.

"What will Thule say?" Ches leaned forward and stared at the firebird. "He put it there, you know. He doesn't like to be thwarted."

The firebird opened one eye and stared sadly at Ches. Lucky came over and stood in front of it.

"Is life there so awful that you must defy Thule?"

The firebird opened both eyes and looked at Lucky, clearly communicating in some secret manner.

Suddenly Lucky laughed. "The firebird is going home."

"That's a relief," Ches said. "I'm not sure if we are up to fighting Fang."

"Her own home, I mean," Lucky said. "Far away, in a volcano, I believe. She was taken from the nest before she hatched and has dreamed of her home all her life."

"Oh, that's wonderful," Susan said. She flung her arms around the firebird's neck. "I'll miss you, but I'm so glad."

"You could always visit, Su. I believe volcanoes are relaxing places to see," Vicky said with a grin.

"What will Thule say?" Cathy said, worried the firebird would get into trouble.

"Thule won't punish his own daughter," Lucky said. "But as the firebird says, he's probably forgotten he left her there all those years ago. I foresee a happy reunion."

"And don't worry, she will leave you with enough feathers to keep you in gold for many lifetimes," Susan said.

"Which only leaves us with one little teeny problem," Ches murmured, "called Fang."

"What about my kingdom?" Paul demanded. He had been looking unhappy during the entire conversation. "Haven't you forgotten about Sylverine?"

"I believe Ches should travel to Kyle," Lucky said. "Who else can beat Sylverine and his magical powers?"

Ches groaned. "Very well, but first you must defeat Fang. My people are dying."

"Better to sort out Sylverine first," Charlie said. "I could fly Ches to Paul's palace. It's much closer than Thule. Saves us returning twice to Thule."

"I'm not sure what you're doing here," the king said. "You have broken the fundamental rule of life, separating your powers like that. You can head off anywhere you like now. Don't let us stop you."

"I thought I was banished from the Rock," Charlie said, looking unhappy. "Not from anywhere else."

"You are no longer welcome in Diamond society," the king said.

"Considering that Charlie's action ultimately saved Crocodile Lake, the guardians and the Diamonds, I think you are being unfair," Lucky said.

"It's not my fault." The king sounded benign. "I did not write the rules, it's out of my hands. Even I am bound by higher laws. Charlie, regrettable as it seems, must leave us."

"So may I go anywhere I wish? Even beyond the Diamond realm?" Charlie said slowly.

"I don't care where you go," the king said. "Lucky, sort out the last few pieces of this mess. I need to return to the Rock. I am weary now." He nodded, and several Diamonds picked up his throne and carried him away.

Cathy flung her arms about Charlie. "Oh no, Charlie!"

Charlie waved away all expressions of concern and upset from his friends. "Now I can go where I like," he said. "I can fly Ches all the way to Thule. I'll even be able to take Susan to visit the firebird in her volcanic home."

"Thank you, Charlie," Susan said, but Cathy did not believe his big smile and apparent cheerfulness.

Lucky's sparkle looked much duller than normal as she stood in front of the firebird.

"You have done so much already that you need do no more. But could you help us defeat the snake?"

The firebird shivered.

"We cannot do it without you," Lucky said. "Don't worry, you will be free to leave Thule any time you wish."

"I'll come with you," Susan said, and softly played her flute, the music cheering Cathy despite her fear of Fang and the terrible punishment Charlie faced.

The firebird must have agreed for Lucky said, "Thank you."

"It won't be enough," Ches said. "The firebird and the serpent are meant to be equal and opposite. Neither can defeat the other."

"She won't be alone," the Diamond said. "You were arguing over whether we should get Sylverine first or defeat Fang. Both cases are urgent. Therefore I suggest, now that you have had some rest, we attend to both. If the firebird would be so kind as to take a few passengers to Thule, Charlie will fly the rest of us to deal with Sylverine." Noticing the look on Cathy's face, she added, "I cannot go to Thule without permission any more than Charlie could. Alan, you have shown yourself useful with Diamond magic, so you should accompany Susan and the firebird. Tremere?"

"I shall go with them," Tremere said instantly.

"Charlie, Ches, and I will find Sylverine," Lucky said.

"Cathy is too weak still to go to either place," Yvonne said. "Don't argue, Cathy, you know you are. I'll stay with her."

Cathy was not too pleased at being left out, but she knew it was true. Besides, she did not want to face Fang again.

Chapter Thirty-seven

THE REGENT

V icky couldn't decide whether she would prefer to see Sylverine being caught or face the fearsome Fang. By the time she decided Thule sounded a more exciting adventure, the firebird had already left. Not too pleased, she clambered into Charlie and sat at his prow.

Before leaving, it was agreed that Charlie should fly directly to Paul's rooftop garden.

"If Reece is in her study, we can talk to her there," Paul said. "I'd like to see her without Slithery, so we could explain what he is."

It was a long flight, and when Paul gave a shout at the sight of his city, Vicky sat up, braving the cold wind, to look out. She could see the gleam of rooftops and the great river that flowed by his capital. Charlie flew as high as he dared in the clouds to avoid suspicious eyes, before dropping down gently to the palace.

Vicky was still shivering from her encounter with so high an altitude.

"I – hhhope we don't have to do that again," she stuttered.

Lucky shot her a quick spark, and she warmed instantly. "Thanks, Lucky."

Charlie landed between beds full of shrubs and miniature trees so that he was hidden from sight of anyone passing by the windows that overlooked the garden. Vicky half-expected palace guards there to greet them but it seemed nobody noticed their arrival. Paul and Lucky slipped into Reece's study while the others waited outside. Within a minute, they had returned.

"She's not there." Paul said. "I guess she is out with her special guard terrorizing the villages. Searching for me."

"We need to find out, but you will be recognised, Paul," Lucky said. "Perhaps Vicky should go."

"If I had Ches's magic cloak, I would," Vicky said. She was eager to explore. From the air, the view of the city, built on a mountain with the palace near its peak, fascinated her. Her only fear was her pale complexion would make her stand out among Paul's people as an obvious stranger.

Ches slowly removed the shiny green cloak from an inner recess in his tunic but to Vicky's disappointment handed it to Paul, and showed him how to activate it.

"You might get lost and keep us here all day," Ches said to Vicky. "The prince should go."

Vicky supposed he had a point.

Lucky did not accompany Paul. Her light shone through the cloak, making him appear as a grey ghostly figure carrying a star, so Paul set off on his own.

"I'll be back as quickly as I can," he promised.

The others hid among the shrubbery, fearful of being discovered without the protection of Paul's presence.

"I wonder if we shall even find Sylverine here?" Ches said.

"Why do you say that?" Charlie asked.

"Undoubtedly he would have known of the plan to demolish the lake. Most likely he would have gone to rendezvous with Abcadarniz."

"Maybe his work in destroying Paul's kingdom isn't done yet," Lucky said.

Despite his promise, it was almost two hours before Paul returned. The sun was tipping the horizon, tinging it with pinks and golds, when Paul appeared without warning before them.

Vicky jumped. "Don't do that."

"Sorry, I forgot. Reece is not here."

"You took two hours to find that out?" Vicky said incredulously.

"Do you know where she has gone?" Lucky said.

"Yes. In search of me apparently. It is believed she is headed towards your land, Lucky, with a large contingent of soldiers, ready to attack." Paul looked uncomfortable as he spoke. "I cannot believe she would do that."

"Don't forget, Sylverine is controlling her," Ches said. He shrank and took on the appearance of a Nuone. "Do I look like him?"

Paul stared. "Not quite as evil. He always keeps his hood over his face...yes, like that. You could fool anyone."

"Good. We may need to."

"Charlie, can you take us back towards Nivram? We will follow the road this time, and watch out for any sign of her," Lucky said.

"She would have reached the woods at the foot of the mountains last night," Paul said.

"In time for the show!" Ches muttered.

"Maybe we should go straight home?" Charlie said. "Though I'd like to see her try to attack the Diamonds!"

"Let us check out those woods first," Lucky said. "I want to talk to Reece. And Paul, if anyone sees us leave, tell them they mistook Charlie for a large bird."

"What type of bird would you like to be, Charlie?" Paul asked, his voice heavily humorous.

"A pigeon," Charlie muttered.

"A golden eagle, the second most magnificent flying creature," Lucky said warmly.

Charlie launched himself off the roof of the palace as she spoke. For a second Vicky felt her stomach lurch as Charlie dropped slightly but then he soared high towards the setting sun.

Once clear of the city, Charlie flew lower in the sky, easily seen if anyone looked up, but the countryside seemed quiet, as though the country people were cowering indoors. If what she heard about Reece and her new special guard was true, Vicky was not surprised. The only people that she saw were a couple of farm hands, leading weary workhorses along the road. None of them looked up at the shadow that flitted above.

Dusk came quickly, and Charlie flew low to follow the roadway. It was dark when he landed by the woods. Vicky was glad to stand on firm ground once more.

"I'll hover above you, if I can" Charlie said. He was slow and awkward on the ground. Lucky hid in Paul's pocket and told them to walk through the woods as if they were heading towards Nivram.

"I'll lead," Paul said. "I know the way."

A heavy silence lay upon the woods, broken only by the crunch of twigs beneath their feet and the occasional scurry of an animal in the undergrowth. Clouds must have gathered to clothe the stars after a glorious sunset, for the darkness was almost complete. Moving through the woods, her arms stretched out to avoid obstacles, Vicky became conscious of a growing dread, the fear a monster would spring at her.

It's all in your mind, she told herself, but she kept as close as possible to Paul and Lucky.

After travelling some way into the wood, they stumbled into a large clearing. The remains of a fire, long since cold, greeted them, and the grass was completely flattened as if a large party had rested there.

"Horse hooves," Ches said quietly, his sharp eyes picking them out. "Fresh, no more than twenty-four hours ago."

"So they were here," Vicky whispered. She hadn't really believed Paul when he said his regent would attack the Rock, but now she did. It was easy to imagine the Nilkens being tossed like hay at the end of these soldiers' swords, and as for Cathy and Yvonne... she didn't like to think about that. It was time they forgot about Sylverine and headed home. "Lucky," she began but Ches made an impatient gesture to her.

"Sssh," he said.

Vicky shut up and listened. At first, she could hear nothing, but after a while a faint keening reached her ears. Somebody was in trouble. Or were they? She glanced back at Ches, but he beckoned her to retreat once more under the cover of the trees. The keening was coming closer.

A minute later a woman stumbled into the clearing. She was young and dressed as a soldier. Her headgear was missing, and her blonde hair fell in tangled tresses about her face. Her uniform was muddy although she still had a sword fastened to her belt. She was moaning quite loudly now.

"Where is he? Where is he? What shall I do if I cannot find him?"

She fell to her knees in the centre on the clearing, her face in her hands.

Vicky expected Lucky to appear but the Diamond remained hidden. Paul took a step forward, but Ches restrained him. Instead, Ches, disguised as a Nuone, walked out from beneath the trees. He did not go directly to her but walked to the perimeter of the glade, his back towards the woman.

She fell silent, her eyes fastened on Ches. Suddenly she rose to her feet and rushed forward. "You're here...alive... you did not desert me."

Ches turned slowly and the woman fell to her knees before him. Vicky inched closer. Still shielded by the trees, she was only a couple of paces behind them.

"What goes on here?" Ches spoke quietly, perhaps to disguise his voice.

"I don't know," she said wretchedly. "When we camped last night, I failed to find you. Then the earth exploded, and all my men ran. The horses, too, were frightened and bolted. Where did you go to, Sylverine?"

"Did I not tell you before I left?"

She shook her head, puzzled. "You were there, then you vanished. After the fire fell from the sky, the soldiers left. Deserted me, their captain. How could they be so cowardly?"

"Do you seek the prince still?"

She was silent for a moment. "Let him go, Sylverine. He can do you no harm. Leave him be."

"Where did I tell you I was going, Reece?"

"You said you wanted to find Paul, but you don't tell me everything." She paused, her eyes fixed on Ches's feet. "You have never called me by my name before. You *are* Sylverine, are you not?" She looked up and rose to one knee.

"No," Ches roared, throwing the hood off his head and standing proudly before her. "I am Ches, last of the Thulians."

In a flash she was on her feet.

"Then die," she shouted, her sword flying out of its sheath into her hand. She raised it to strike even as Ches still held his head high.

Two things happened very quickly. Vicky dived at Reece and pushed the regent with all her strength, and out of the corner of her eye, she saw a bright spark flash at the same time and bury itself in the woman's shoulder.

"Ah," she cried, her sword clattering out of her hand and falling to earth some distance away, while Vicky's powerful shove knocked her off her feet and she went sprawling across the moss, Vicky on top of her.

"Reece, Reece, it's me, Paul," the prince shouted, running to her side.

Reece looked at him blankly. Then her gaze travelled once more to Ches. "You will die! All of you will die!"

"Look how dilated her eyes are," Ches said, one foot on the regent's arm while Vicky held her other. An angry foot aimed a vicious kick at him that he easily sidestepped. "Sylverine has her deep in his control."

"Can you free her?" Lucky asked from Paul's shoulder.

"Yes, the magic is only side one." He fumbled among his pockets. "Interesting that despite his enchantment, she still tried to protect Paul. She must be very fond of you, Paul."

"Release me!" the regent shouted.

Ches produced a small silver box that hung off a short metal chain. This he started to swing gently in front of Reece's eyes.

"Get that out of my face, fiend," Reece said. "Your magic won't work on me."

"Watch it," Ches said. "Follow the silver."

"Never," she muttered but her eyes started to follow the moving object all the same.

As Ches spoke words in a strange language, the regent's limbs began to relax, though Vicky kept a firm grip on her all the same. Soon Reece's eyes were closed, and she slept.

"She'll wake shortly," Ches said, snapping the object back into his pocket. "Back to herself, whatever that is."

"Where are her soldiers?" Vicky said. "Do you think they really ran away?"

Paul snorted. "Miserable pack of scoundrels, cowards and bullies."

A groan came from the woman on the ground. She opened her eyes, and her glance fell on the prince. "Paul?"

"Yes, it's me, Reece. You are all right now. Sylverine's spell has been broken."

"What do you mean?" She looked suspiciously at his companions. "Release me."

Vicky let go and stood back.

Reece looked at Charlie, who had landed at the edge of the clearing, and her face darkened. "You."

"Last time we met, we did have words, I admit," Charlie said, not visibly upset. "With hindsight, I realise that perhaps you were already under the influence of another."

"Where is Sylverine?" Reece interrupted him and got to her feet. She noticed her sword lying a few feet away and went to get it. Vicky looked at Lucky, but the Diamond made no sign.

"We thought you could tell us," Paul said.

Reece picked up her sword and twirled it a few times before shoving it into its sheath.

"Why are we here, Paul? I don't remember."

"We don't have time for explanations," Lucky said. "Paul can fill you in later. But if you don't know, then I suspect Sylverine either tried to join Witch Rose in her castle or is slipping back to Thule as we speak."

Reece looked at Lucky. "I'm sorry I cannot tell you where he went. I remember his voice, always poisoning my ears, but more than that I don't recall."

"We'll take you back to the palace," Lucky said. "Then Charlie and I will travel to Thule, with Ches and Vicky, of course, and see if we can find him."

"Thule," Vicky said. "Maybe we'll be in time to fight the snake?" She was not sure if she hoped they would or not.

"With a bit of luck," Charlie said with a wink.

Chapter Thirty-eight

BATTLING FANG

The firebird flew quickly and directly across Nivram. She did not seem to mind carrying Susan, Alan, and Tremere, and flew as gently and carefully as she could. Her back was warm, a good antidote to the cold air that burned against their faces, but despite the harness that Lucky had set up so that her passengers could sit in safety on her back, it was an uncomfortable journey.

"You're so much faster than Charlie," Alan said as they landed on the cliffs overlooking the sea, not far from Zania. "He took the best part of the day to get here. You've done it in a couple of hours." He wanted to pat the firebird but was a little nervous that he would upset her.

"Less than two hours, I'd say," Tremere said. "It's good to stretch our legs. I wonder how the others are getting on in their search for Sylverine?"

They walked for a short while and found a stream. The firebird refused to drink, but Tremere topped up the water skins. They sat down for a while in the sun and ate some food. Alan had warned them that a long sea voyage lay ahead.

"We left our boat on an island out in the bay," Alan said, glad they were flying this time. "Charlie said it was the last island of the Diamond realm. I feel bad about the boat."

"We can collect and return it another time," Tremere said. "First let us concentrate on the task in hand."

Alan had been thinking of nothing else.

After the firebird had rested for a while, it was time to move on.

"What will we do once we get there?" Susan said.

"If it's true that your friend here can match the serpent," Tremere said, "perhaps she can hold him while we attack. That is the only plan I have, but I am open to suggestions." As Susan mounted the firebird's back, Tremere turned to Alan. "Your sisters have magical gifts, all of them. Have you none?"

Alan gripped one of the ropes to help him climb up. "No." Tremere seemed to wait for more, so he continued with, "I lost it," before quickly hauling himself up.

Tremere swung himself up behind him. "I have had the strangest dreams recently. Like a memory coming back to me from years ago in Lowdar. A small boy gives me something to mind. I can't recall what it is, but I know it is valuable." The firebird flapped its wings and Tremere had to shout to make himself heard. "I think that boy was you, Alan."

Alan said nothing. For a moment his hopes leapt that the gift from his dying mother would soon be returned to him, but then he decided that it was unlikely, and even if he had given it to Tremere to look after (so he wasn't so stupid as to misplace it after all), his uncle had lost everything. Alan's gift was still missing. Lucky had promised to help him recover it, and he was happy to wait for her. In the meantime, he gazed down at the sea below, which stretched in a blue-grey sheet as far as he could see.

It wasn't long before the last island of the Diamond realm appeared below. The boat had taken most of the day to reach Thule. He wondered how long it would take the firebird.

Maybe the breeze was behind it, but the firebird flew like the wind. Before Alan realised how close they were, the yellow-white cliffs of Thule appeared on the horizon. He nudged Susan and pointed. She nodded in comprehension, though she looked rather pale.

From the air, Alan could better appreciate the size of the desert, and how it stretched in three directions. Dune after dune passed beneath the firebird before finally the valley of the city opened before them.

The golden lake, the city gleaming in the evening sun, and a great serpent coiled about its base.

The firebird landed on the soft sand, close to where Alan and Cathy had first seen the city. Alan dismounted in a hurry and felt for Charlie's chip.

I'm ready for you, he thought. *You'll be sorry you hurt Cathy.*

Susan stroked the firebird's face, making soothing noises. Then she took out her flute and played a few bars of a tune. The firebird perked up at the sound, raised her head, and nudged Susan's arm.

Tremere gave each of them a few instructions and they set off. Alan noticed Susan fidgeting with her flute a lot. He wondered how she planned to use it.

The coils that wound about the island seemed even thicker than Alan remembered. Fang's head was not visible, it had to be watching one of the other gates. The bridge that should have crossed the lake to the west gate was missing. Some crumbling masonry on the shore was all that was left.

Fang watched the south gate. The golden gates stood wide open and Nuones teemed anxiously about the entrance. Occasionally the great serpent lunged and the Nuones scattered, only to regroup once Fang lowered its head. The bridge at the south gate was still standing, though large gaps in the stonework made it impossible to cross. If Fang had devoured the bridge at the north side, the Nuones had little hope of escape.

Several small boats bobbed in the water quite close to the south gate, tied to a support of the bridge. They were within jumping distance of the gate, and probably a safer means of crossing the lake than the crumbling bridge. No wonder the Nuones were tempted to make for them. Yet Alan had the feeling that Fang was teasing them with the boats, hoping to snatch them in the air as they jumped.

Susan resumed her seat on the firebird. "I know you want me to stay back," she said to Tremere, "but she wants me with her."

"Very well, be careful." Tremere looked at Alan. "Ready?"

Alan nodded, and clutched Charlie's chip even harder.

The giant serpent noticed the firebird as she trembled by the shore, Susan patting her. It lost interest in the Nuones, and with a loud splashing sound and a groan of falling stone, began to unwrap himself from the city.

"It's coming after us." Alan hadn't expected that. He stared at the numerous coils of snake wrapped about the island. Fang was a ferocious and enormous foe.

"Quick," Tremere urged. "Now."

The firebird opened her mouth and released a small spurt of fire. If Alan had been standing directly in front, he would have been scorched. On the snake, a hundred paces away, it made no impression.

Fang quickened the unwrapping of its body.

The firebird emitted another feeble flame.

Fang had loosened itself sufficiently to stretch its head close to the shore.

"Fall back," Tremere said, his sword at the ready.

Alan moved back to a safer distance. Susan, perched on top of the firebird, could not follow. Alan glimpsed a flash of silver, and the flute was out once more and to her lips. The strains of a haunting melody issued from the flute. Fang paused, momentarily, before proceeding. It opened his mouth to bite the firebird, but Alan flashed Sparkie at it and the beast hesitated. In that moment, the firebird pulled herself together, flapped her wings and rose into the air, out of reach.

Alan's momentary relief changed to horror as Fang kept coming, its attention riveted on Alan. Standing his ground, he aimed, imploring Sparkie to stop Fang. A dazzling ray of light shot at the snake. At the same time, the firebird swooped again and this time flame from a mighty furnace burst over its head.

Fang halted, its hide damaged by the firebird's scorching attack. Tremere ran up to Fang and hacked at its eyes. The serpent turned to snap at Tremere's head, but Alan directed a searing burn that made Fang roar, while the firebird homed in with another mighty blast of fire.

After the third attack, Fang had enough. Pus poured from its eye and half its face was blackened to ash. Thick skin hung in strips from its head. It turned and dived under the water, the last few coils of its body unwrapping from the island.

"It's getting away," Alan yelled. "Let's get after it."

Fang disappeared beneath the golden waters of the lake. Aware of the cheering Nuones at the gate, Alan recalled how they had thrown him and Cathy into the dungeons, a death sentence over their heads, yet he was still glad to free them from Fang.

The firebird was not finished. She wheeled about in the sky, turned and dived fast and sped over the water, trailing fire as she went. The lake burst into flames. With an angry roar, Fang exploded out of the water, covered in flames from head to tail. It rolled and squirmed upon the sand, but its body continued to blaze. Blackened and charred, the monster eventually fell back and stopped moving.

The lake was still burning but the flames were dying.

And Fang was dead.

Chapter Thirty-nine

BACK TO THE PALACE

A gleam of late evening sun broke out from behind a cloud and fell upon the roof garden of the palace. Paul had arranged for lanterns to be placed around a table, and all were already lit. A fine spread was laid, some dishes on special warming pans, others under covers. Paul had sent away the servants. He wanted his visitors all to himself.

A speck in the sky announced Charlie's approach, and a few minutes later, the flying canoe came to rest in the roof garden. Cathy and Alan, Vicky, Susan, and Yvonne all climbed out, while Lucky's sparkle announced her presence. After exchanging greetings, the guests took their places at the table.

"Uncle Matt sends his apologies," Yvonne said. "He had to visit the Forest men."

"That's a pity," Paul said. "I told him it would only be us."

It was a couple weeks after Fang's defeat. Ches had returned to Thule. Their recent fright had sparked the Nuones into making an effort to live in harmony with each other. Few had fallen victim to Fang, and they were grateful to their rescuers, who were promised the freedom of the city on their next visit. In the meantime, the Nuones had to rebuild their bridges, repair damaged walls, and get over the loss of their mascot.

The firebird had eventually flown home but promised to be back. And as Charlie had said, he could always fly Susan, and anyone else, to its far distant land to visit.

Sylverine never turned up in Thule. Either he had perished in the destruction of the witch's castle or had slunk off to some other hideout. The Diamonds had put out enquiries. If he were still alive, sooner or later he was bound to turn up.

"How about Reece?" Vicky asked. "Is she normal again?"

Paul nodded. "It's like the old days. But better. She includes me more now. I am learning more and more about my country and the lives of my people. All those foreign soldiers have left, and I have my old guard back. Tomorrow is a public holiday for the whole country. Our first since my father's coronation."

"That's wonderful," Lucky said. "Sounds like there are no lasting repercussions from Sylverine's interference."

"If he hadn't tried to destroy us, I'd probably be still in the classroom learning stuff," Paul said. "Reece says she realises now that I am old enough to... to find out what is really going on." He was pleased how things had turned out. It almost made his kidnapping worth it. *Almost*.

"We have some news," Cathy said, her eyes dancing excitedly as she nudged Alan. "Tremere has been looking after Alan's gift all these years, and he remembered what it was just before we left."

Paul was delighted to hear this, and judging by the gasps from Cathy's sisters, they hadn't known this news either. The twins had waited until Paul was present before they revealed it. No one had bothered doing anything like that for him before.

"Show them, Alan," Cathy said.

Alan took out a piece of leather and carefully unrolled it to reveal a dagger with a stained blade and rusted handle.

Tremere's dagger that cut through his chains so easily! Paul almost laughed. He should have guessed it was magic.

"Shall I remove the miasma that hides its true appearance, Alan?" Lucky said.

Alan nodded vigorously. "Yes please."

A spark flew from Lucky and wiped away the rust, revealing a beautiful silver dagger with an ornate handle. Alan picked it up and pressed it to his cheek. "I remember you," he whispered.

"It's beautiful," Susan said. Vicky gave a whoop, and Yvonne grinned happily.

"Is it from Thule as well?" Cathy said,

"We'll need Dulstar to confirm but I expect so," Lucky said.

For a few minutes they talked about the dagger, and Paul reminded them of his experience in the prison.

"In the right hands, it can cut anything," he declared.

"Isn't it weird none of us can remember it?" Vicky said, picking up a biscuit.

"You must have given it immediately to Uncle Matt," Yvonne said. "We were too upset over Mama..." Her voice trailed off.

Paul sipped from a large silver goblet and decided to change the subject. "When is the wedding? I thought it would have taken place by now."

"The wedding is off," Charlie said.

"For the moment," Lucky quickly added. "You know how awkward my father is... but in a few more days, he will realise his mistake and apologise to you, Charlie."

"Of course he will," Susan said.

"He did before," Cathy said.

"Sure," Charlie said. "But take your time planning your outfit, everyone. It may be a while."

"We are staying the night with you, aren't we, Paul?" Yvonne said as the sun set in a glorious panoply of colour.

"My quarters await," Paul replied. "Entry via either the door or the window. You may choose your preferred method."

They sat in silence for a while, watching the colours fade from the sky. Insects buzzed about the colourful lanterns and Susan produced her flute and played a melancholic air. Even though Queen Rose had been defeated, and Fang destroyed, Charlie's predicament had taken much of the pleasure from their victory. After all, if he had not given Alan a sliver of himself containing all his powers, the twins would not have met Ches, or survived Fang. The Diamonds would not have emerged from their home in time to stop the witch...in short, Charlie had a done a great service to the Diamonds, Nivram, Thule and Paul's kingdom.

But Paul knew how erratic the King of the Diamonds was. It did not surprise him that he had banished Charlie once more, but he was equally certain that the king would soon forgive and forget. Charlie's banishment would be of short duration.

He stood up. "I propose a toast." Everybody looked at him and raised their glasses expectantly. "To Charlie and Lucky," Paul pronounced solemnly. "And their future happiness."

EPILOGUE

The small dark body lay prone upon the ground, unmoving for days.

At first the moss, which thickened on the forest floor, grew over its limbs and tried to claim it as their own, but something about the inert figure made it slip away almost as quickly.

Then the forest mist gathered about, hoping to absorb its spirit, but it found the body essence distasteful and hastily moved on.

The trees ducked their branches and gently caressed it. They had long memories and recognised it as their own, even though it did not move.

On the nineteenth day, the body stirred.

It was alive.

AUTHOR'S NOTE

When the King of the Diamonds banished Queen Rose from Nivram for a thousand years, I didn't expect we would hear from her again. Not so soon. And definitely not with a world-wreaking or Diamond-destroying plan, all executed from her floating castle so that technically she *didn't* return to Nivram. I love spending time with the children, Lucky, Charlie and the Diamonds, and I had fun with their new friends, Ches and the firebird, but I really hope Queen Rose's trouble-making days are finally over.

Yet somehow I feel we will hear from her again.

I hope you enjoyed reading *Revenge of Queen Rose*. I'd love to know what you thought of it. Please visit my website valinoratr oy.com for more information about Nivram, my books and me, and you can use the contact page there to send me a message. I reply to all readers who get in touch!

It would be awesome if you would tell your friends about the book or leave a review in Amazon, Goodreads or any book review site. A few lines would be great, and it also helps other readers discover the world of Nivram.

Special thanks to my cover artist, Elizabeth Eckstein, for another fabulous cover, and to Joseph Sale for editing this book. Thanks to my family and friends for putting up with me over the last few months as I worked on this book, and especially to my dog who didn't get as many walks as he was promised.

SIGN UP TO MY READERS NEWSLETTER!

Sign up to my readers club occasional newsletter and get news of upcoming releases, updates on my writing, and learn more about Nivram and other fun stuff. Simply scan on the QR mark below for the sign up page. *If you are under 13, please ask a grown-up to sign up for you.*

As a welcome, I'll send you a FREE eBook of my short story collection *Once Upon A Time.*

This free collection features a mythical water dragon, an overworked dragon put up for sale, a boy who make a bad deal with a puppet master, and a girl who needs the help of a dog and a bird to find her father in a retelling of *Beauty & the Beast.*

ABOUT THE AUTHOR

Valinora Troy has been writing since she was a child. Her first story popped into her head when she was 5 or 6, about a little girl who found a magic diamond.

Recently she completed a M.A. in Creative Writing, specialising in Children & Young Adult fiction. Her short stories for adults have appeared in numerous venues. She hails from Blackrock, Co Louth, Ireland, and after living in Dublin for a number of years, recently returned to a magical writing cottage in the Louth area.

Revenge of Queen Rose is her second published novel.

Printed in Great Britain
by Amazon